TOMBSTONE TWINS
SOUL MATES

STONE ARCH BOOKS
a capstone imprint

Stone Arch Books
1710 Roe Crest Drive, North Mankato, Minnesota 56003
www.capstonepub.com

Cataloging-in-Publication Data is available on the Library of Congress website.
ISBN (hardcover): 978-1-4342-2248-0
ISBN (paperback): 978-1-4342-3873-3
ISBN (e-book): 978-1-4342-6097-0

Summary: Dedbert doesn't fit in at Underworld Elementary. He died flushing himself down the toilet, and now he's the butt of all butt jokes. Then one day, a new student, Skully, arrives. And guess what? She's Dedbert's death twin – they died in the exact same way! These two quickly become friends, and discover that they truly are Tombstone Twins. Soul mates.

Printed in the United states in Stevens Point Wisconsin. 092012 006937WZS13

Ashley C. Andersen Zantop . . . . PUBLISHER
Michael Dahl . . . . EDITORIAL DIRECTOR
Donald Lemke . . . . EDITOR
Heather Kindseth . . . . CREATIVE DIRECTOR
Bob Lentz . . . . ART DIRECTOR
Brann Garvey . . . . SENIOR DESIGNER

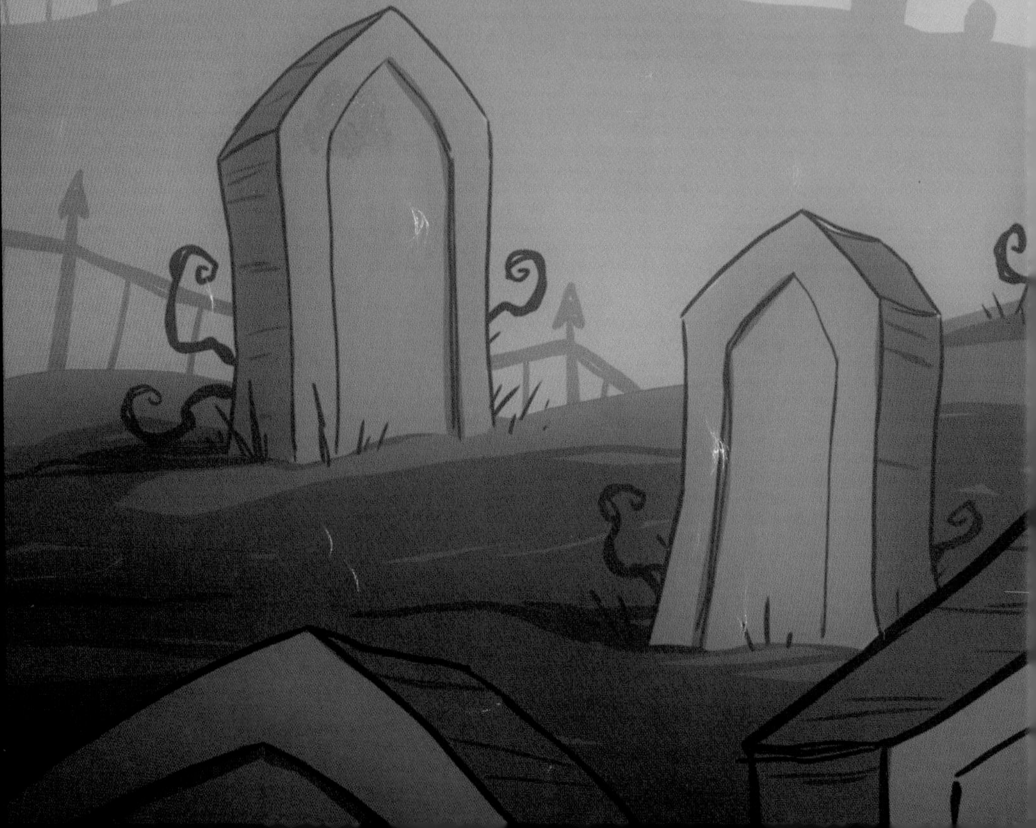

TOMBSTONE TWINS

SOUL MATES

WRITTEN BY
DENISE DOWNER

ILLUSTRATED BY
OTIS FRAMPTON

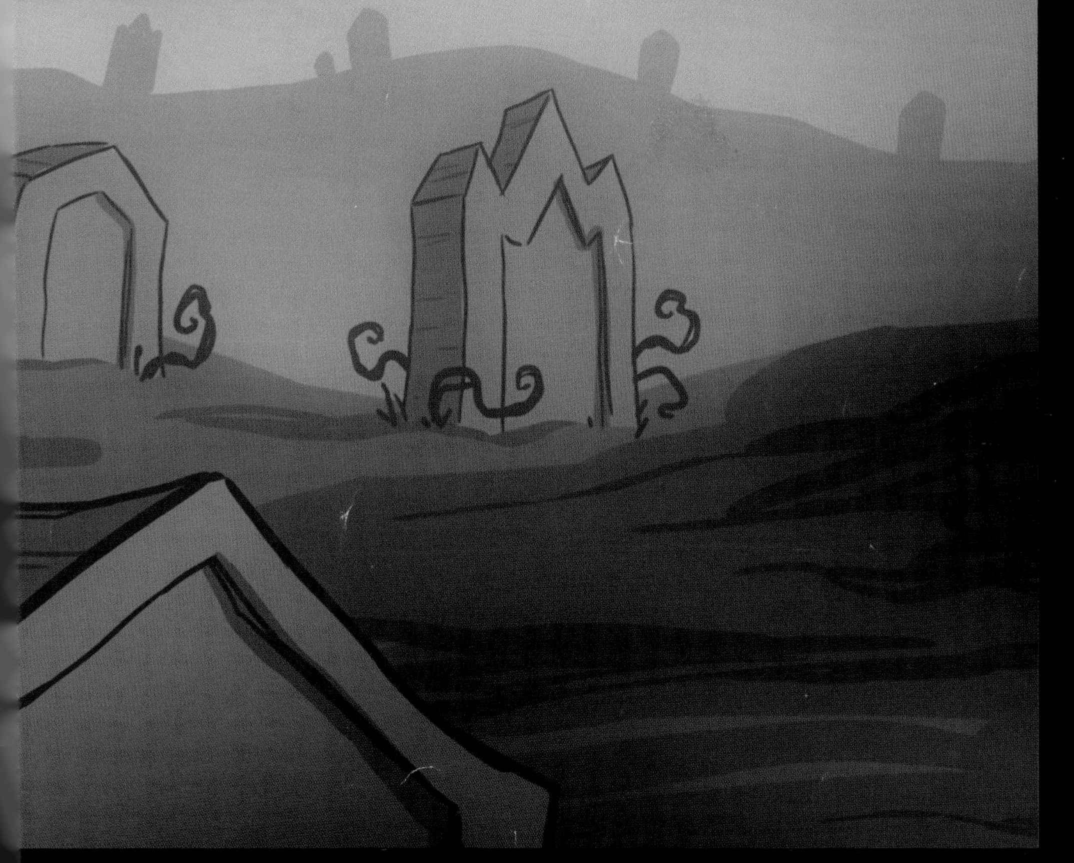

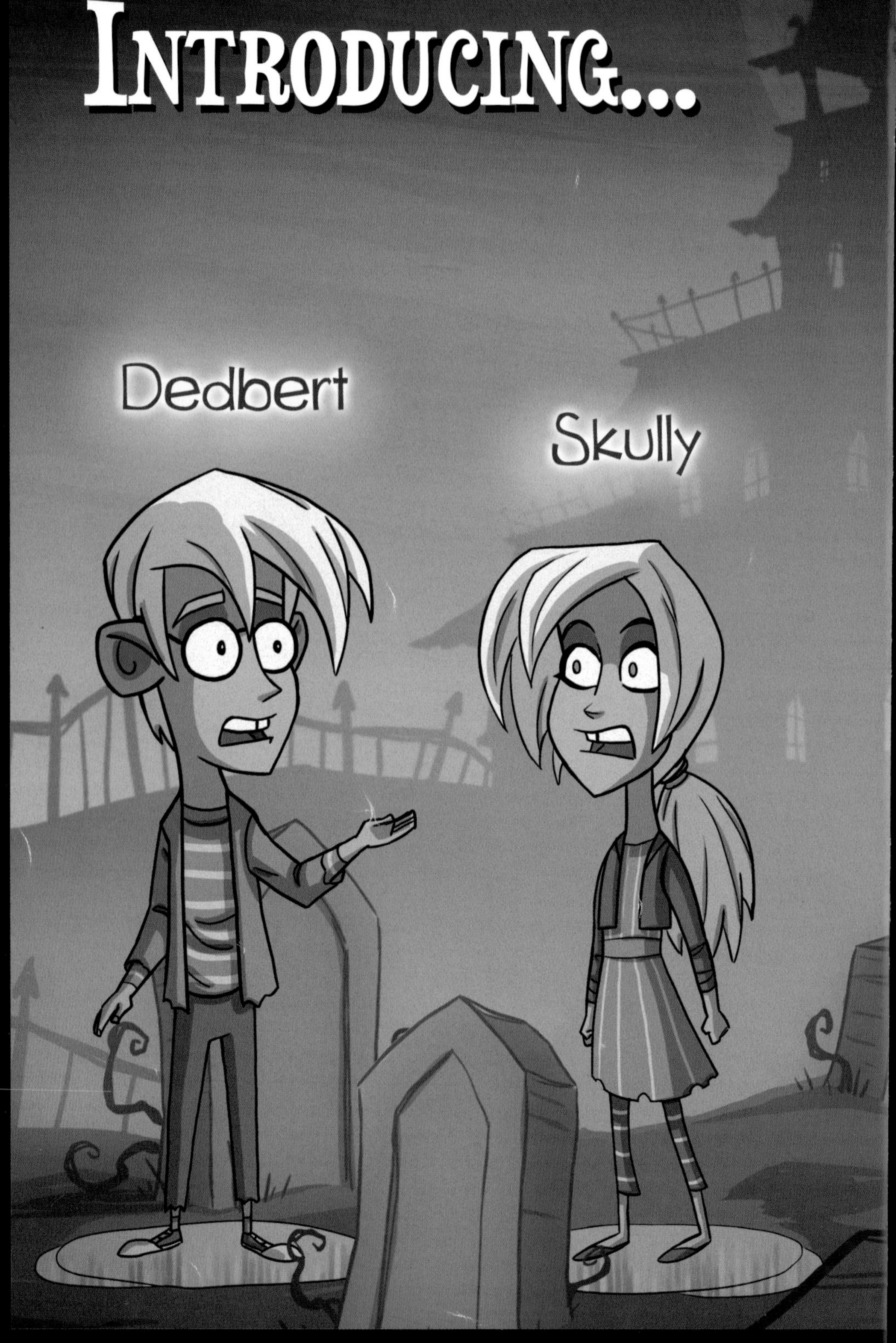
INTRODUCING...
Dedbert
Skully

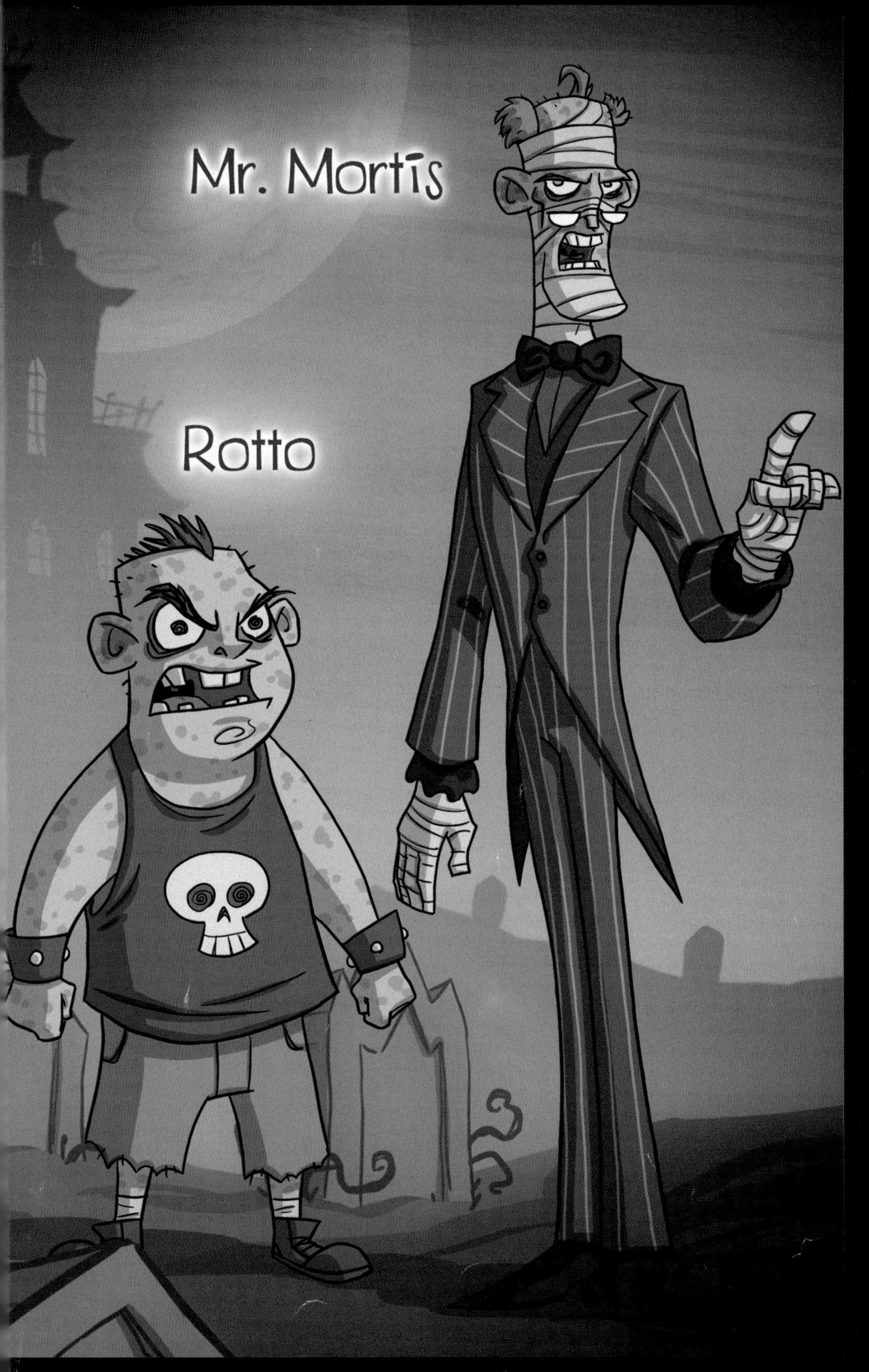
Mr. Mortis
Rotto

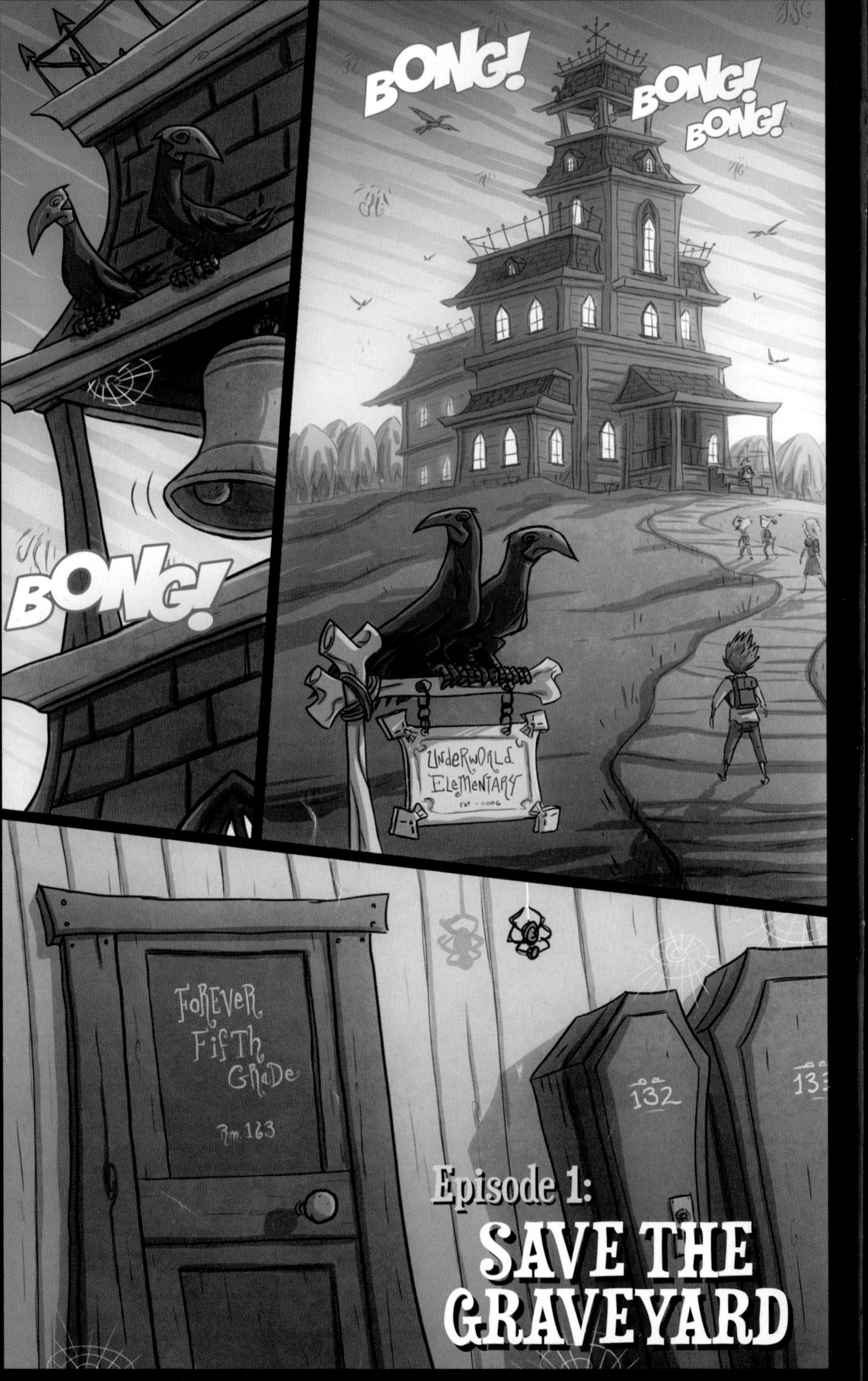
BONG!
BONG!
BONG!
BONG!
UnderWorld Elementary
Forever Fifth Grade
Rm. 163
132
Episode 1:
SAVE THE GRAVEYARD

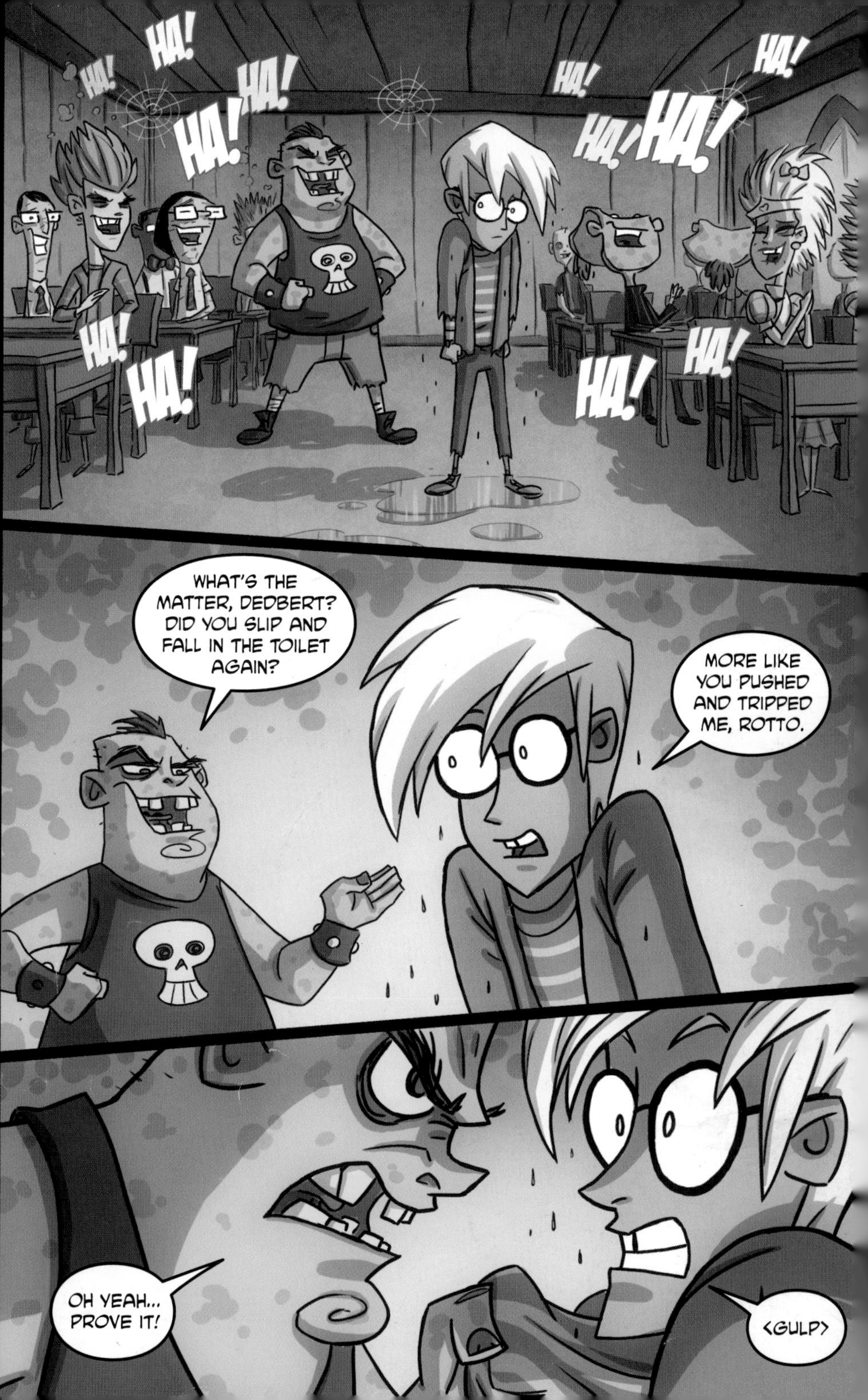
HA!
HA!
HA!
HA!
HA!
HA!
HA!
HA!
HA!
HA!
HA!
HA!
WHAT'S THE MATTER, DEDBERT? DID YOU SLIP AND FALL IN THE TOILET AGAIN?
MORE LIKE YOU PUSHED AND TRIPPED ME, ROTTO.
OH YEAH... PROVE IT!
<GULP>

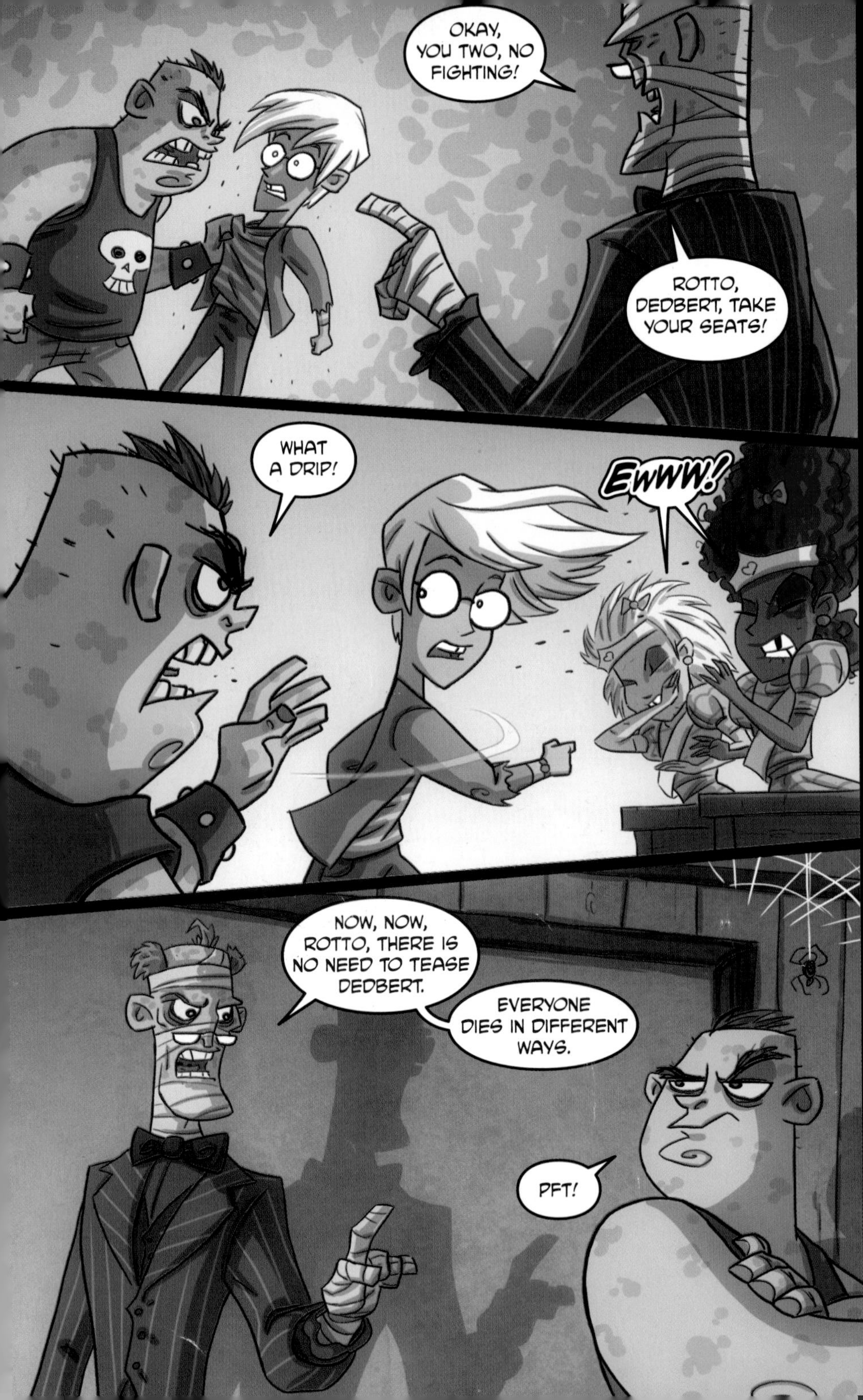
OKAY, YOU TWO, NO FIGHTING!
ROTTO, DEDBERT, TAKE YOUR SEATS!
WHAT A DRIP!
EWWW!
NOW, NOW, ROTTO, THERE IS NO NEED TO TEASE DEDBERT.
EVERYONE DIES IN DIFFERENT WAYS.
PFT!

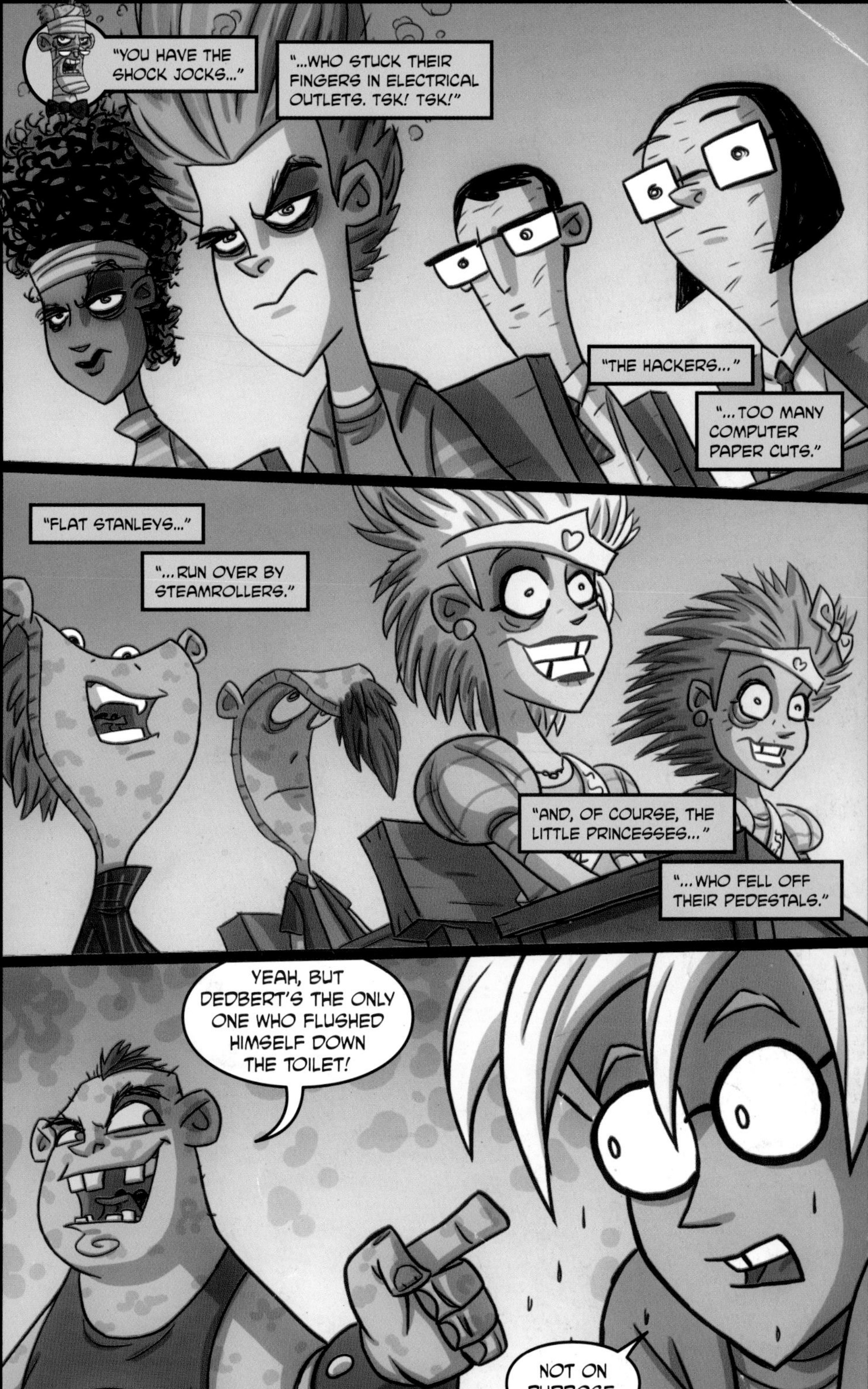

"YOU HAVE THE SHOCK JOCKS..."
"...WHO STUCK THEIR FINGERS IN ELECTRICAL OUTLETS. TSK! TSK!"
"THE HACKERS..."
"...TOO MANY COMPUTER PAPER CUTS."
"FLAT STANLEYS..."
"...RUN OVER BY STEAMROLLERS."
"AND, OF COURSE, THE LITTLE PRINCESSES..."
"...WHO FELL OFF THEIR PEDESTALS."
YEAH, BUT DEDBERT'S THE ONLY ONE WHO FLUSHED HIMSELF DOWN THE TOILET!
NOT ON PURPOSE.

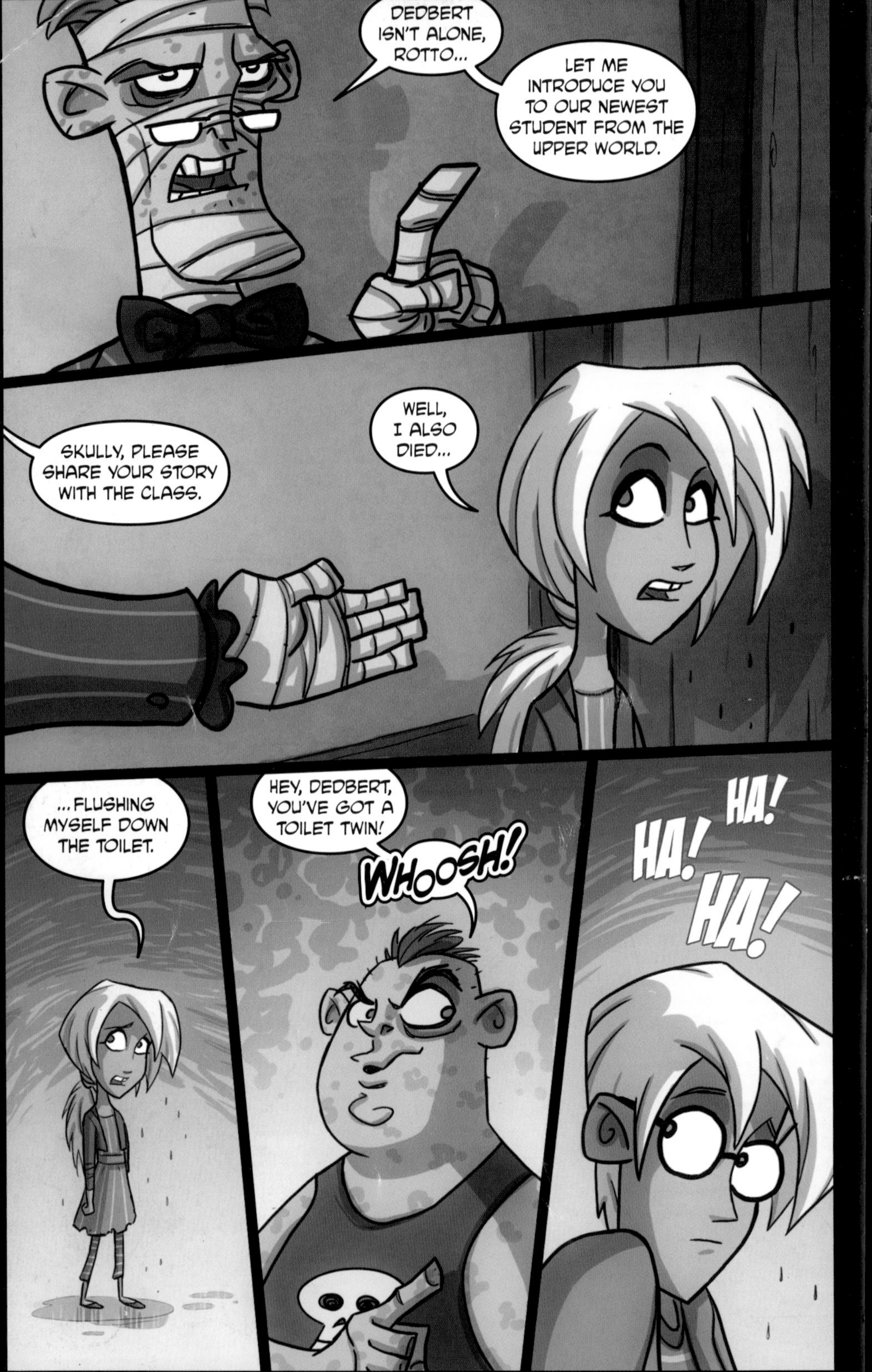
DEDBERT ISN'T ALONE, ROTTO...
LET ME INTRODUCE YOU TO OUR NEWEST STUDENT FROM THE UPPER WORLD.
SKULLY, PLEASE SHARE YOUR STORY WITH THE CLASS.
WELL, I ALSO DIED...
...FLUSHING MYSELF DOWN THE TOILET.
HEY, DEDBERT, YOU'VE GOT A TOILET TWIN!
WHOOSH!
HA! HA! HA!

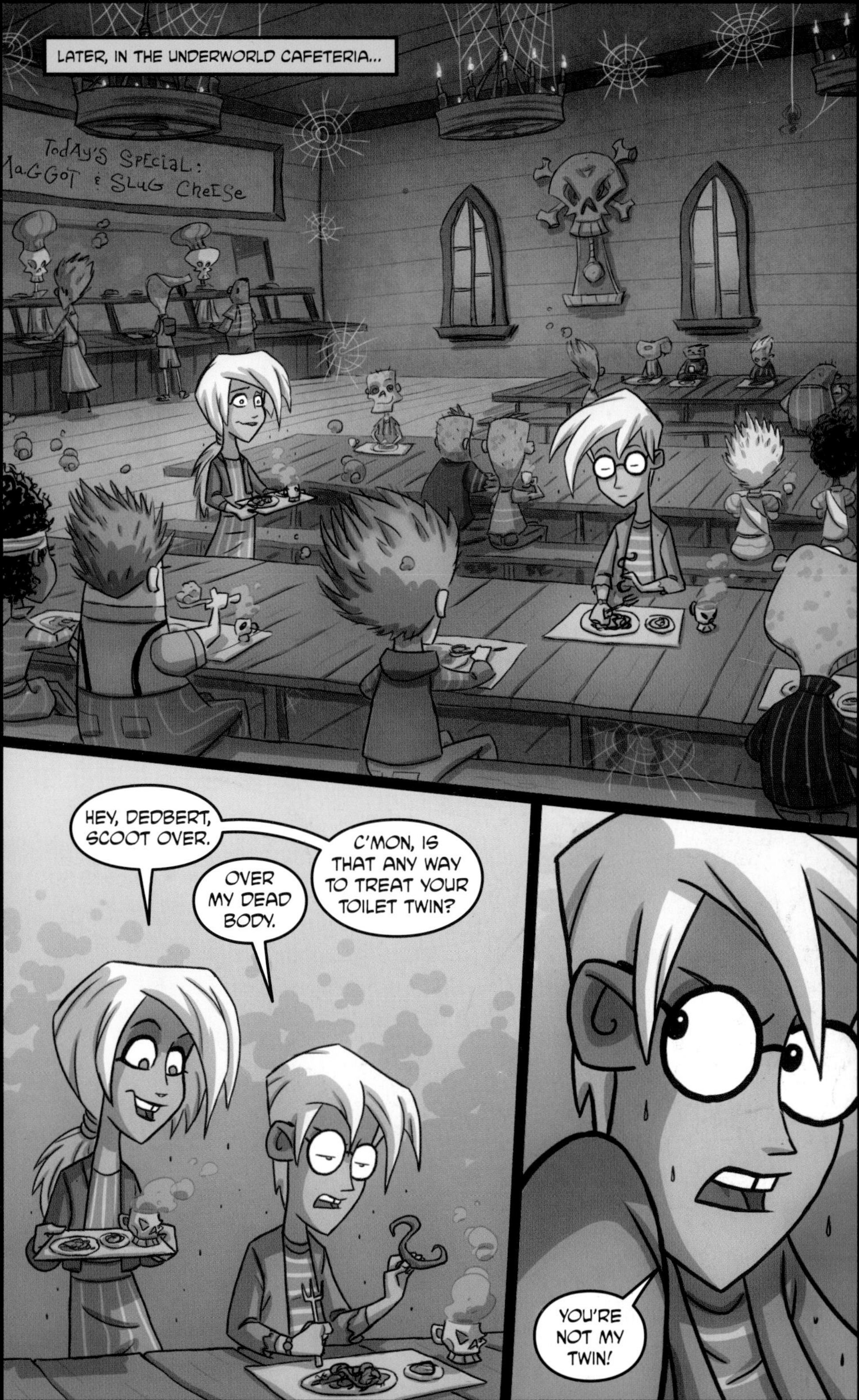

LATER, IN THE UNDERWORLD CAFETERIA...
TODAY'S SPECIAL: MaGGOT & SLUG CHEESE
HEY, DEDBERT, SCOOT OVER.
OVER MY DEAD BODY.
C'MON, IS THAT ANY WAY TO TREAT YOUR TOILET TWIN?
YOU'RE NOT MY TWIN!

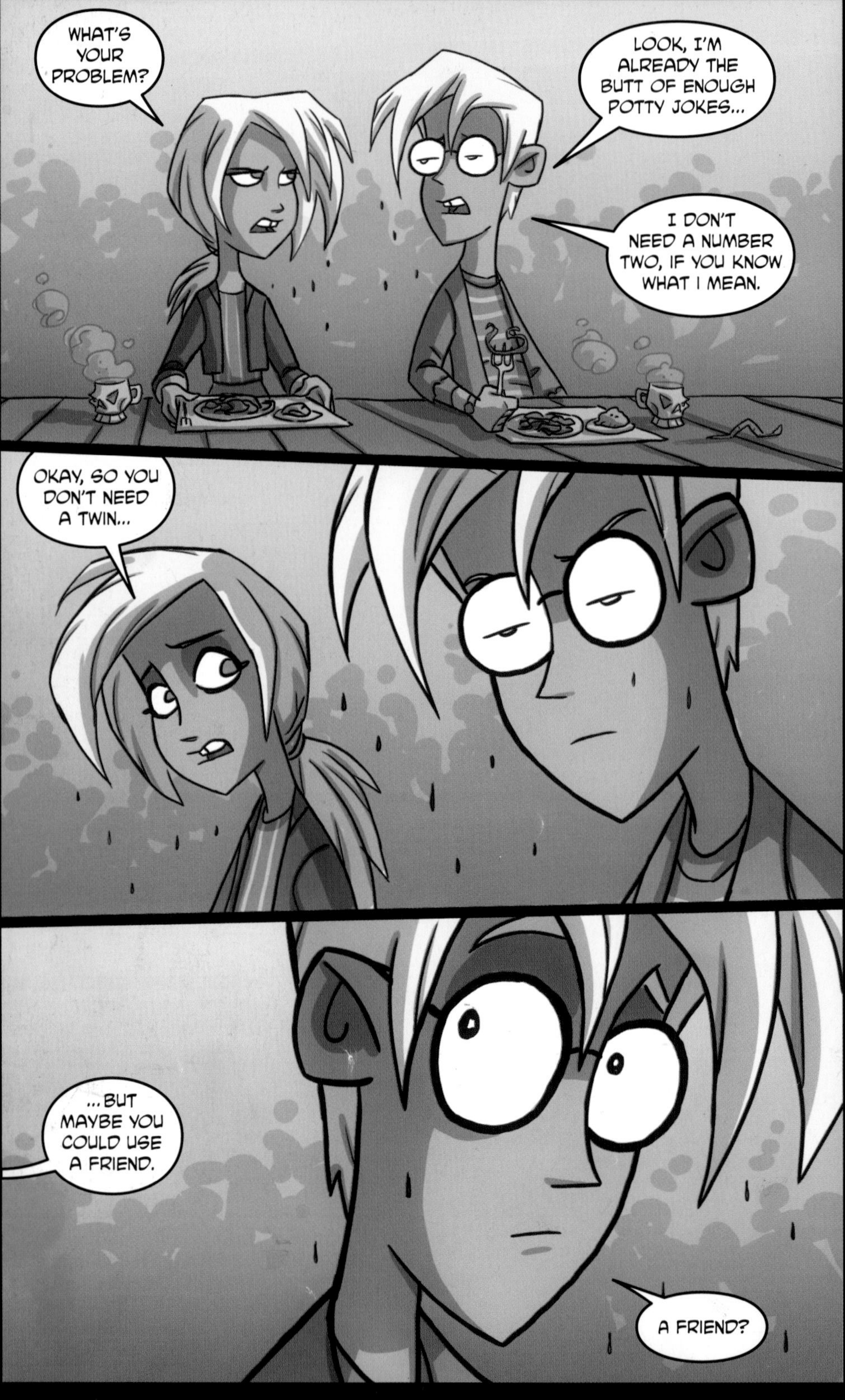
WHAT'S YOUR PROBLEM?
LOOK, I'M ALREADY THE BUTT OF ENOUGH POTTY JOKES...
I DON'T NEED A NUMBER TWO, IF YOU KNOW WHAT I MEAN.
OKAY, SO YOU DON'T NEED A TWIN...
...BUT MAYBE YOU COULD USE A FRIEND.
A FRIEND?

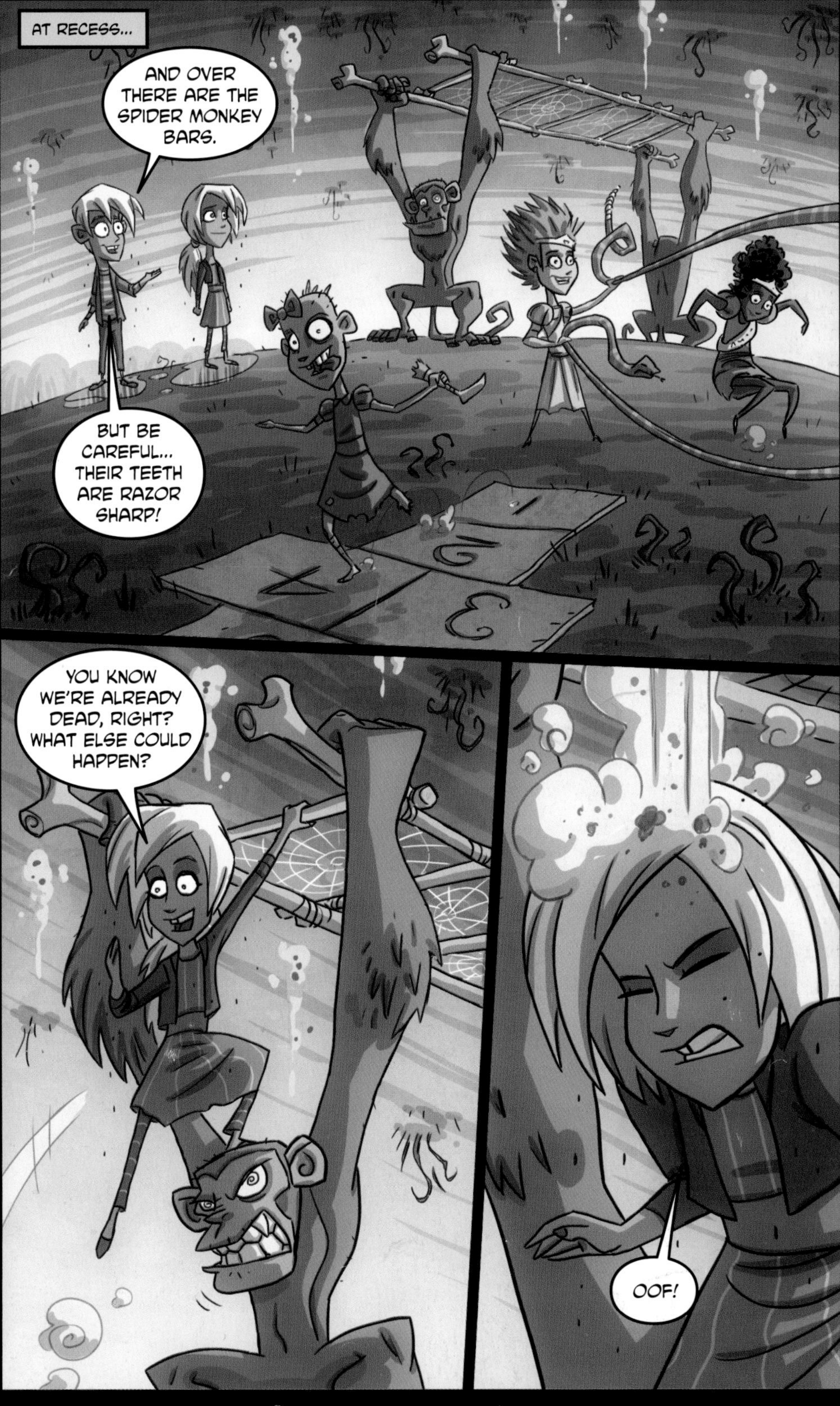
AT RECESS...
AND OVER THERE ARE THE SPIDER MONKEY BARS.
BUT BE CAREFUL... THEIR TEETH ARE RAZOR SHARP!
YOU KNOW WE'RE ALREADY DEAD, RIGHT? WHAT ELSE COULD HAPPEN?
OOF!

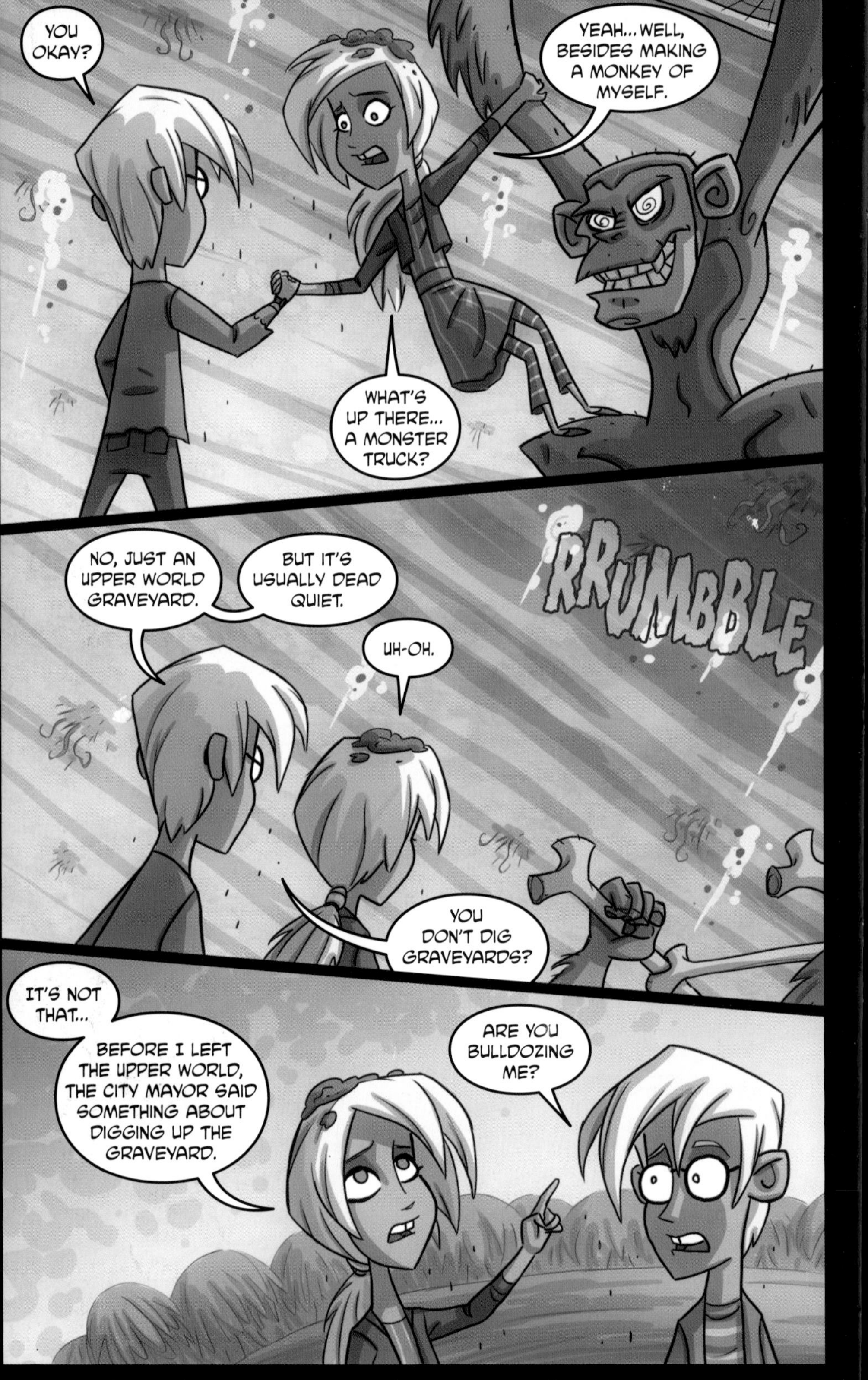
YOU OKAY?
YEAH... WELL, BESIDES MAKING A MONKEY OF MYSELF.
WHAT'S UP THERE... A MONSTER TRUCK?
NO, JUST AN UPPER WORLD GRAVEYARD.
BUT IT'S USUALLY DEAD QUIET.
RRUMBBLE
UH-OH.
YOU DON'T DIG GRAVEYARDS?
IT'S NOT THAT...
BEFORE I LEFT THE UPPER WORLD, THE CITY MAYOR SAID SOMETHING ABOUT DIGGING UP THE GRAVEYARD.
ARE YOU BULLDOZING ME?

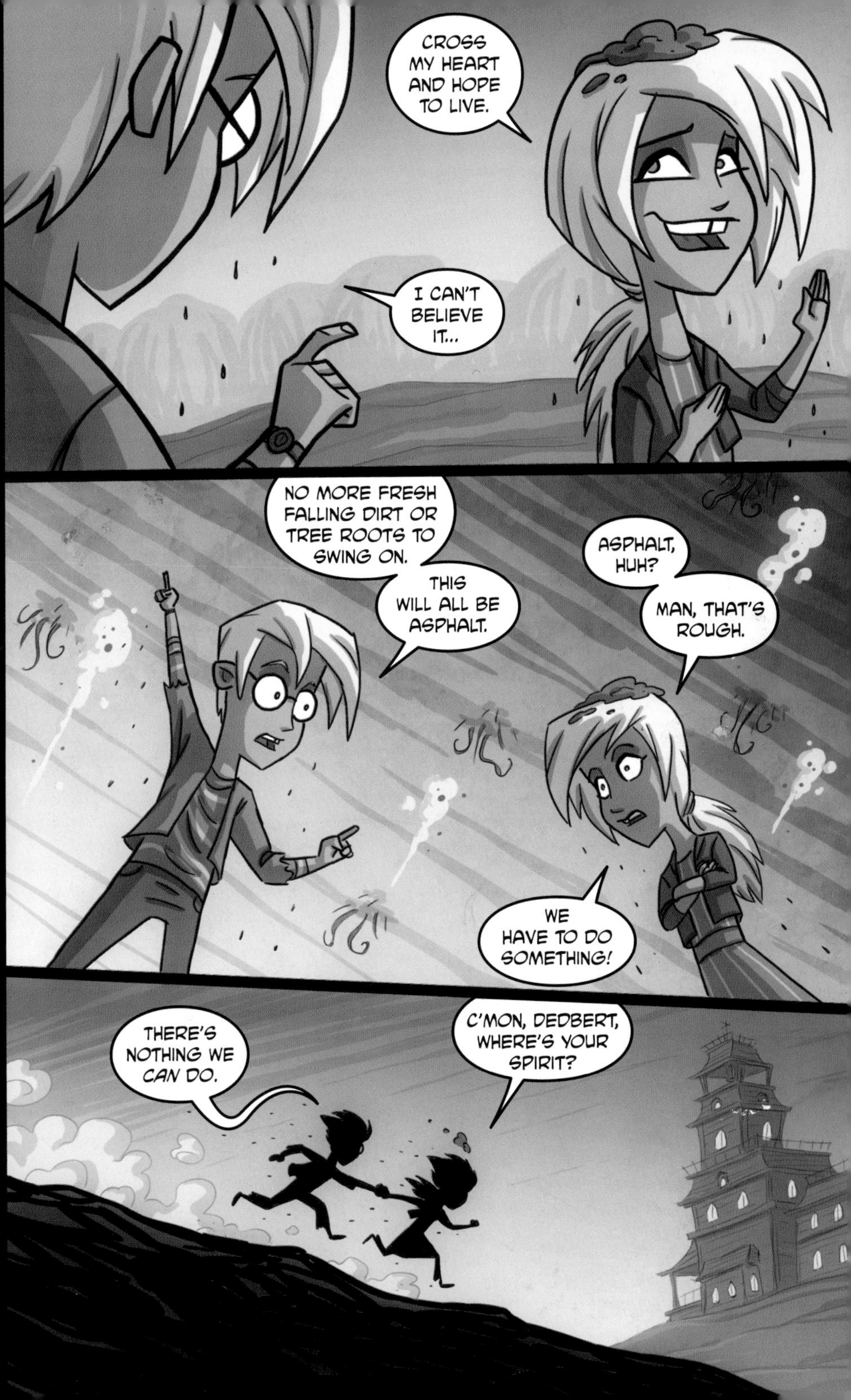

CROSS MY HEART AND HOPE TO LIVE.
I CAN'T BELIEVE IT...
NO MORE FRESH FALLING DIRT OR TREE ROOTS TO SWING ON.
THIS WILL ALL BE ASPHALT.
ASPHALT, HUH?
MAN, THAT'S ROUGH.
WE HAVE TO DO SOMETHING!
THERE'S NOTHING WE CAN DO.
C'MON, DEDBERT, WHERE'S YOUR SPIRIT?

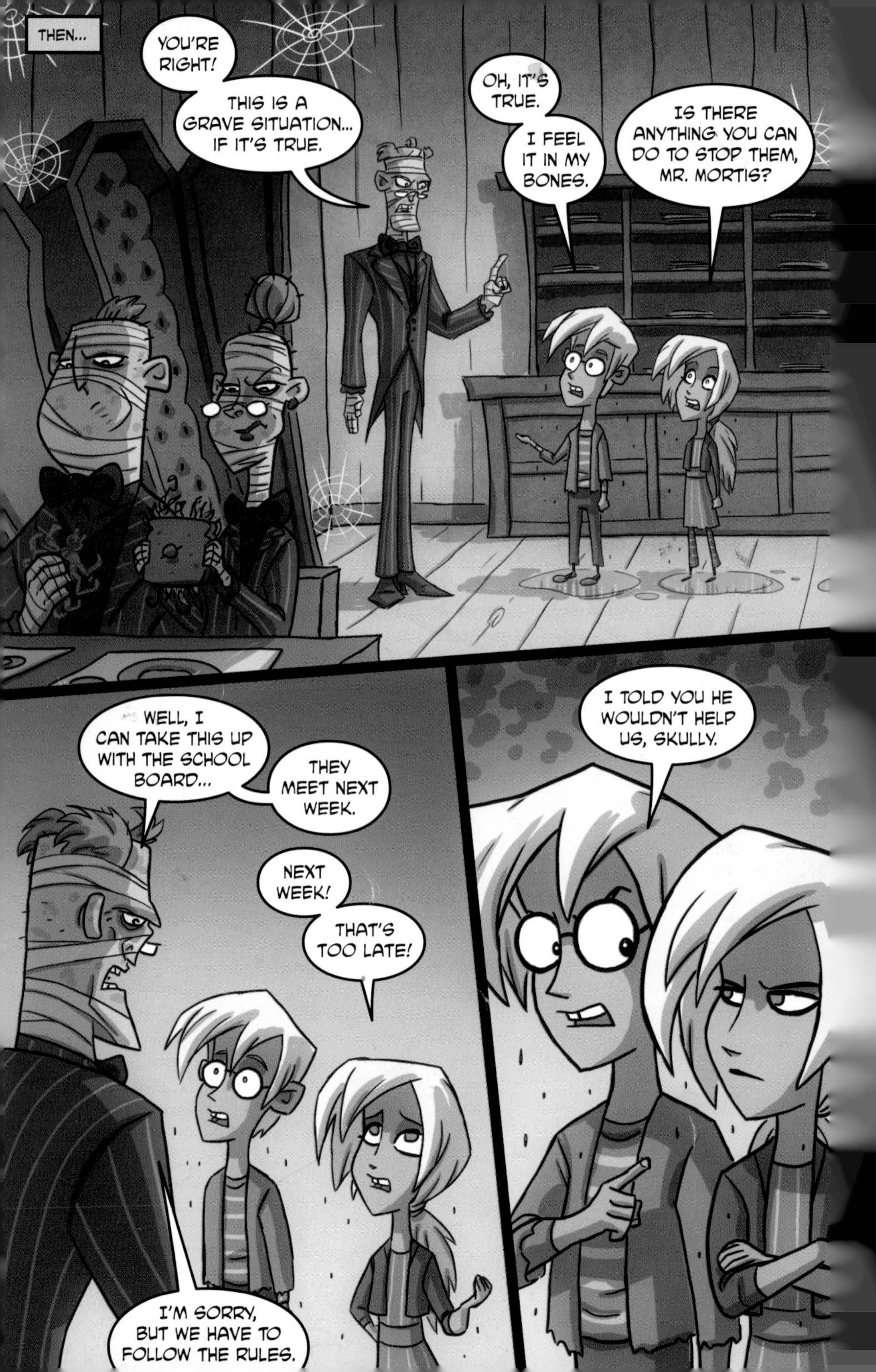
THEN...
YOU'RE RIGHT!
THIS IS A GRAVE SITUATION... IF IT'S TRUE.
OH, IT'S TRUE.
I FEEL IT IN MY BONES.
IS THERE ANYTHING YOU CAN DO TO STOP THEM, MR. MORTIS?
WELL, I CAN TAKE THIS UP WITH THE SCHOOL BOARD...
THEY MEET NEXT WEEK.
NEXT WEEK!
THAT'S TOO LATE!
I'M SORRY, BUT WE HAVE TO FOLLOW THE RULES.
I TOLD YOU HE WOULDN'T HELP US, SKULLY.

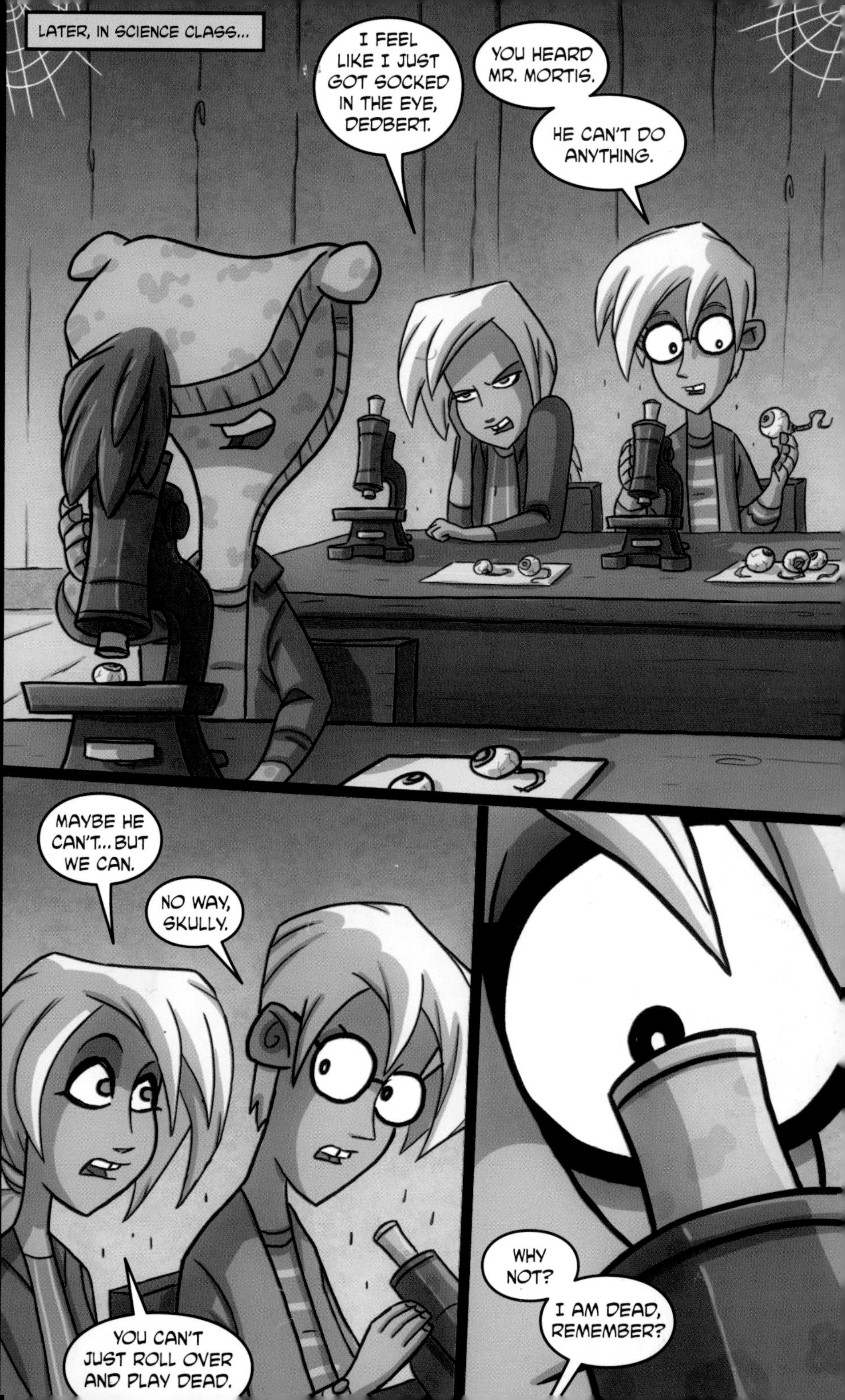
LATER, IN SCIENCE CLASS...
I FEEL LIKE I JUST GOT SOCKED IN THE EYE, DEDBERT.
YOU HEARD MR. MORTIS.
HE CAN'T DO ANYTHING.
MAYBE HE CAN'T... BUT WE CAN.
NO WAY, SKULLY.
YOU CAN'T JUST ROLL OVER AND PLAY DEAD.
WHY NOT?
I AM DEAD, REMEMBER?

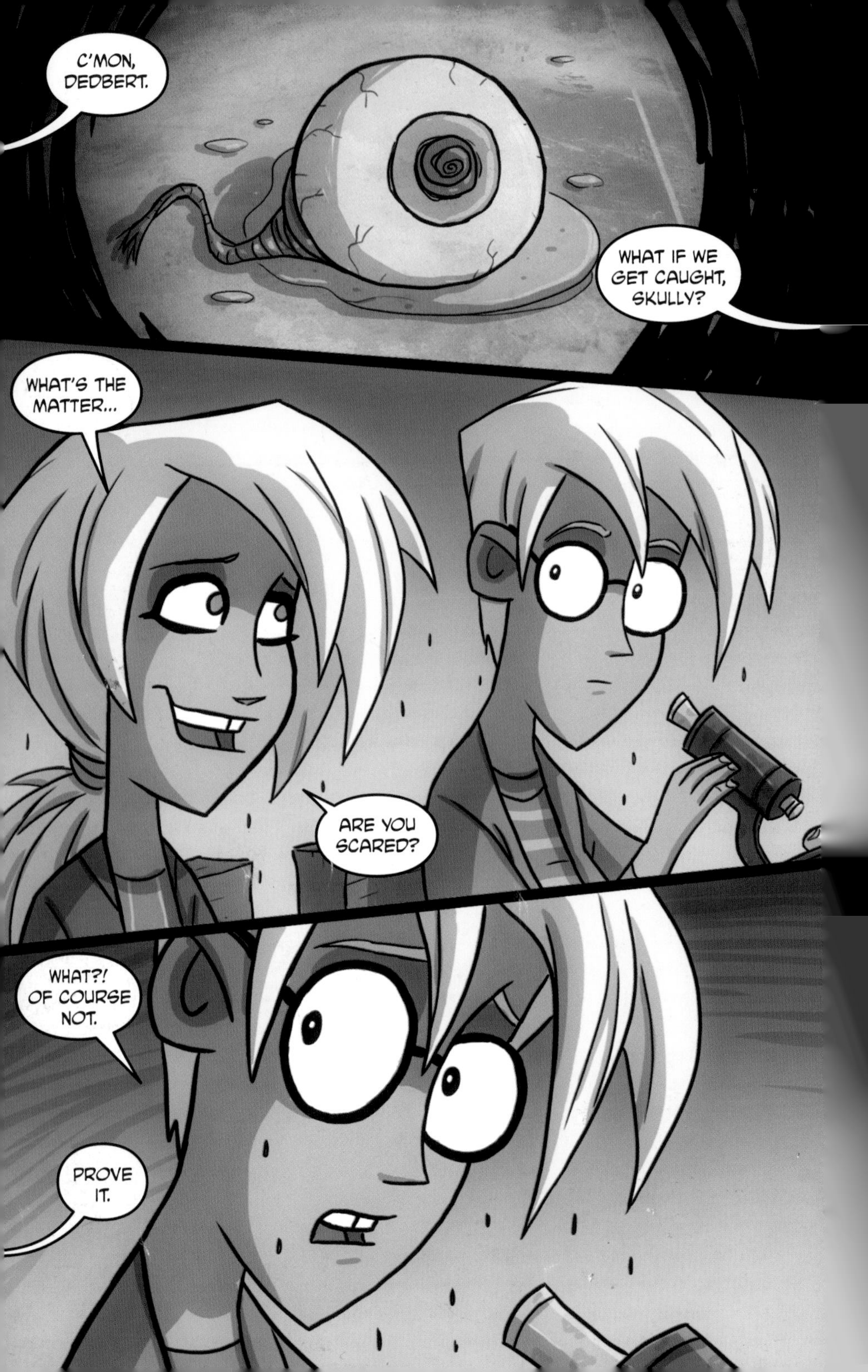
C'MON, DEDBERT.
WHAT IF WE GET CAUGHT, SKULLY?
WHAT'S THE MATTER...
ARE YOU SCARED?
WHAT?! OF COURSE NOT.
PROVE IT.

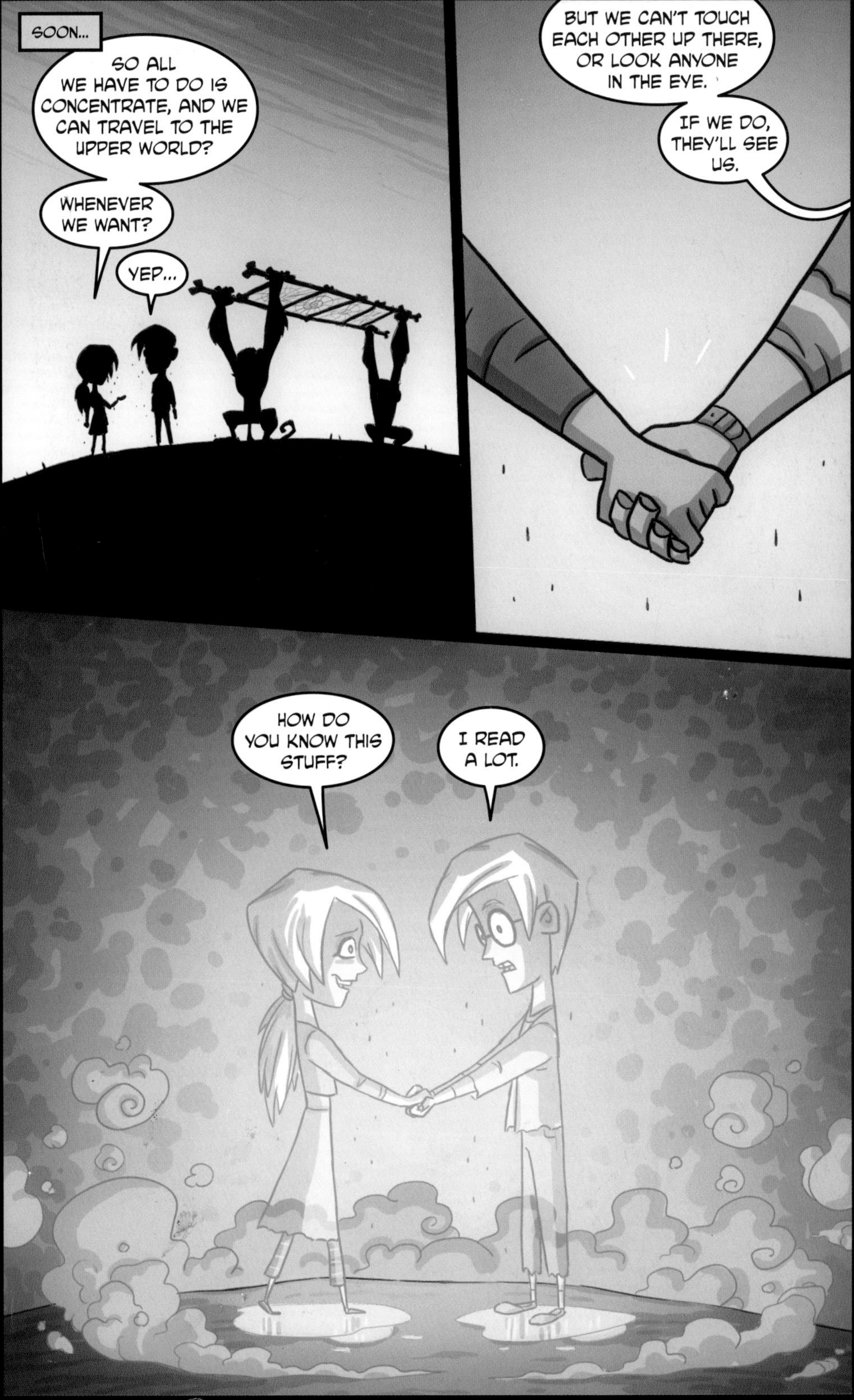
SOON...
SO ALL WE HAVE TO DO IS CONCENTRATE, AND WE CAN TRAVEL TO THE UPPER WORLD?
WHENEVER WE WANT?
YEP...
BUT WE CAN'T TOUCH EACH OTHER UP THERE, OR LOOK ANYONE IN THE EYE.
IF WE DO, THEY'LL SEE US.
HOW DO YOU KNOW THIS STUFF?
I READ A LOT.

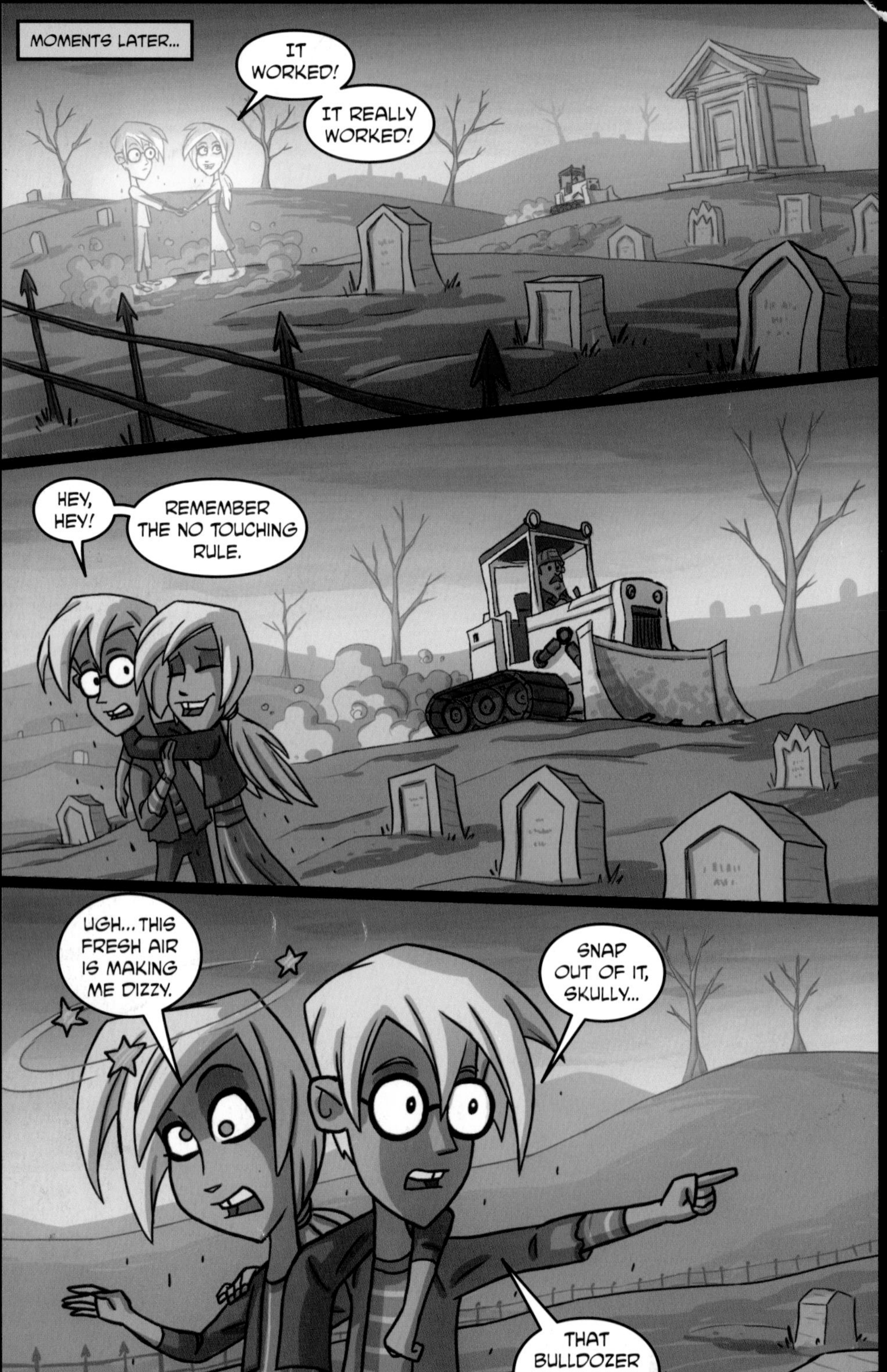
MOMENTS LATER...
IT WORKED!
IT REALLY WORKED!
HEY, HEY!
REMEMBER THE NO TOUCHING RULE.
UGH... THIS FRESH AIR IS MAKING ME DIZZY.
SNAP OUT OF IT, SKULLY...
THAT BULLDOZER IS HEADED THIS WAY!

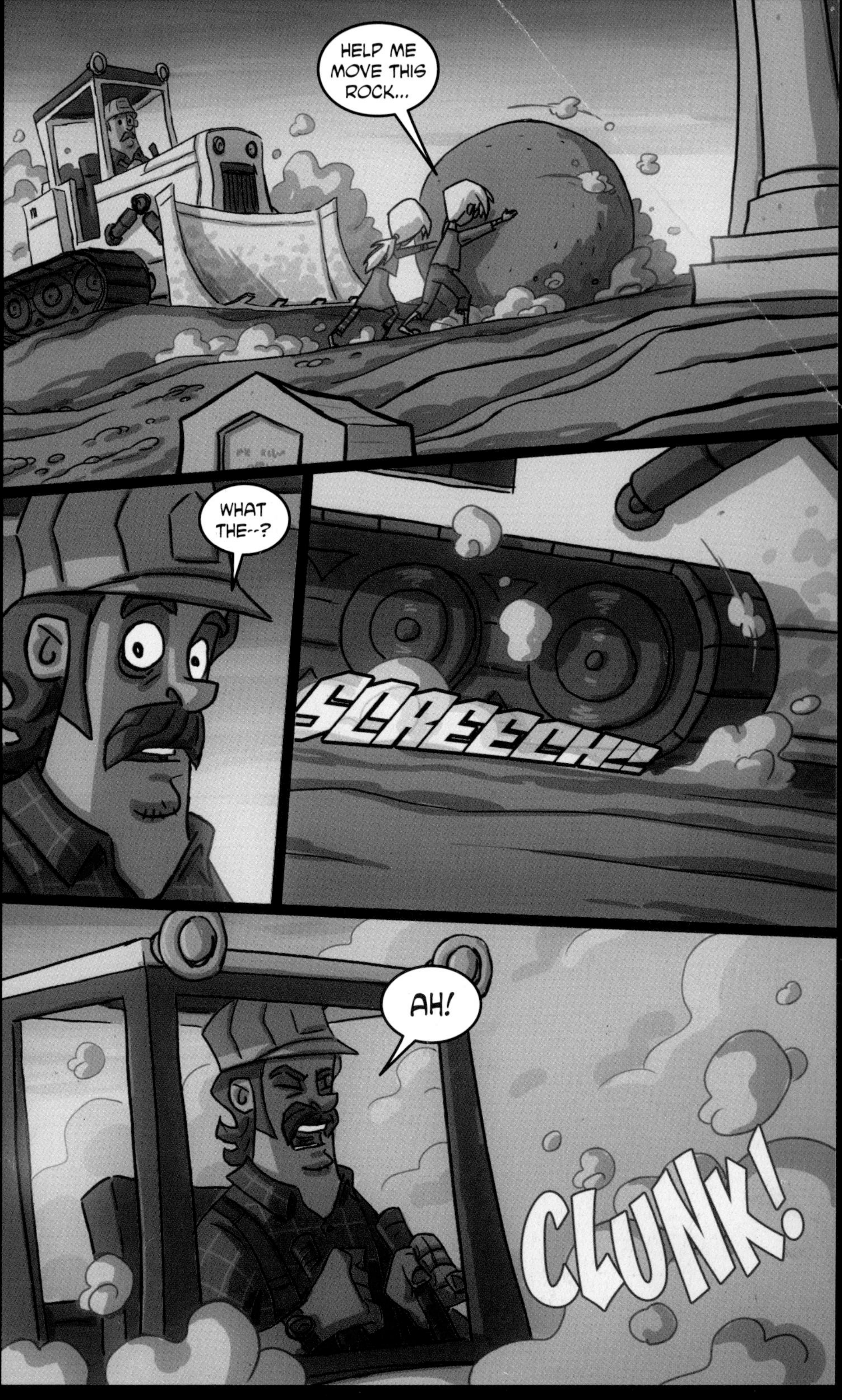
HELP ME MOVE THIS ROCK...
WHAT THE--?
SCREECH!!
AH!
CLUNK!

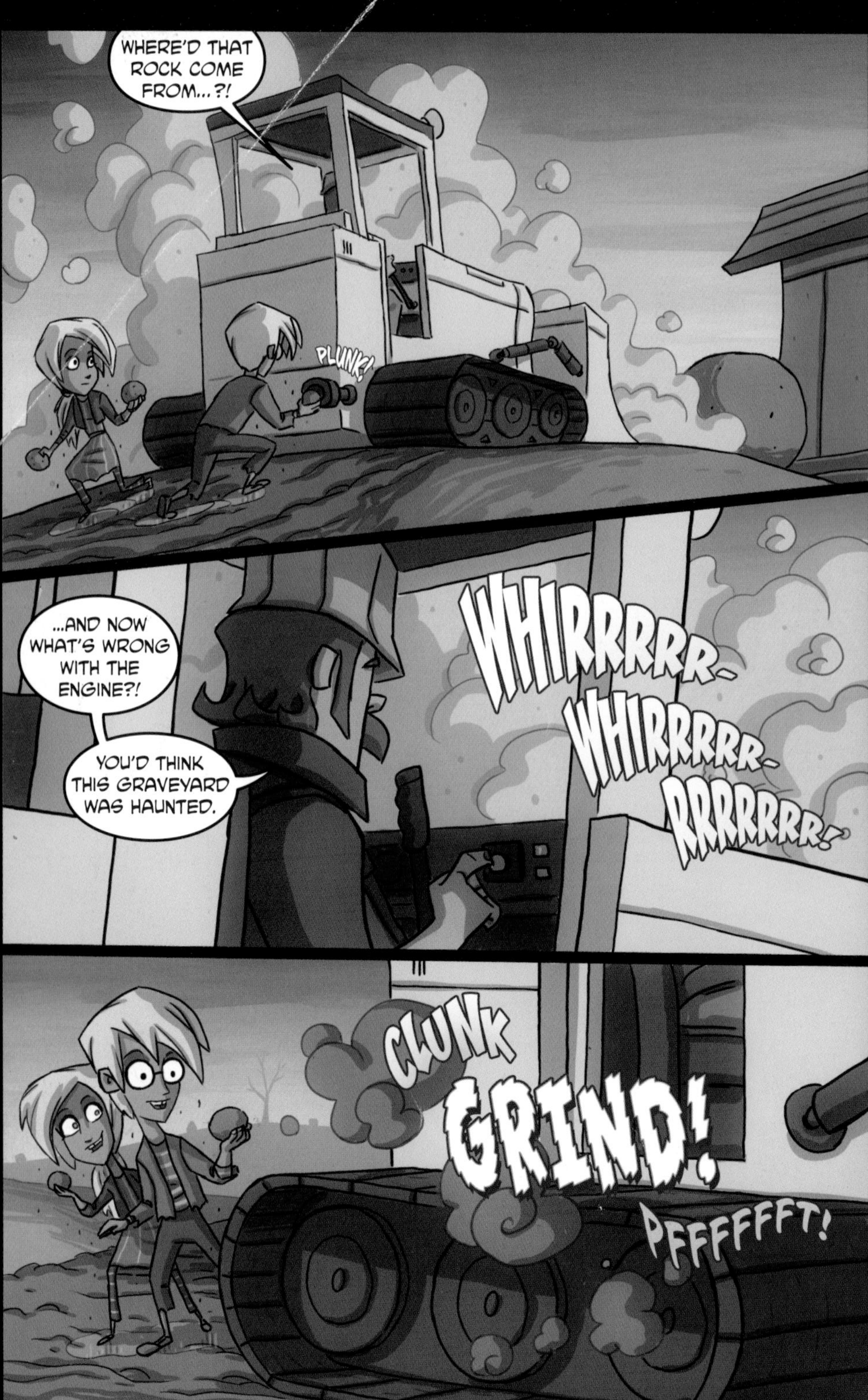
WHERE'D THAT ROCK COME FROM...?!
PLUNK!
...AND NOW WHAT'S WRONG WITH THE ENGINE?!
YOU'D THINK THIS GRAVEYARD WAS HAUNTED.
WHIRRRRR-WHIRRRRRR-RRRRRRR!
CLUNK
GRIND!
PFFFFFT!

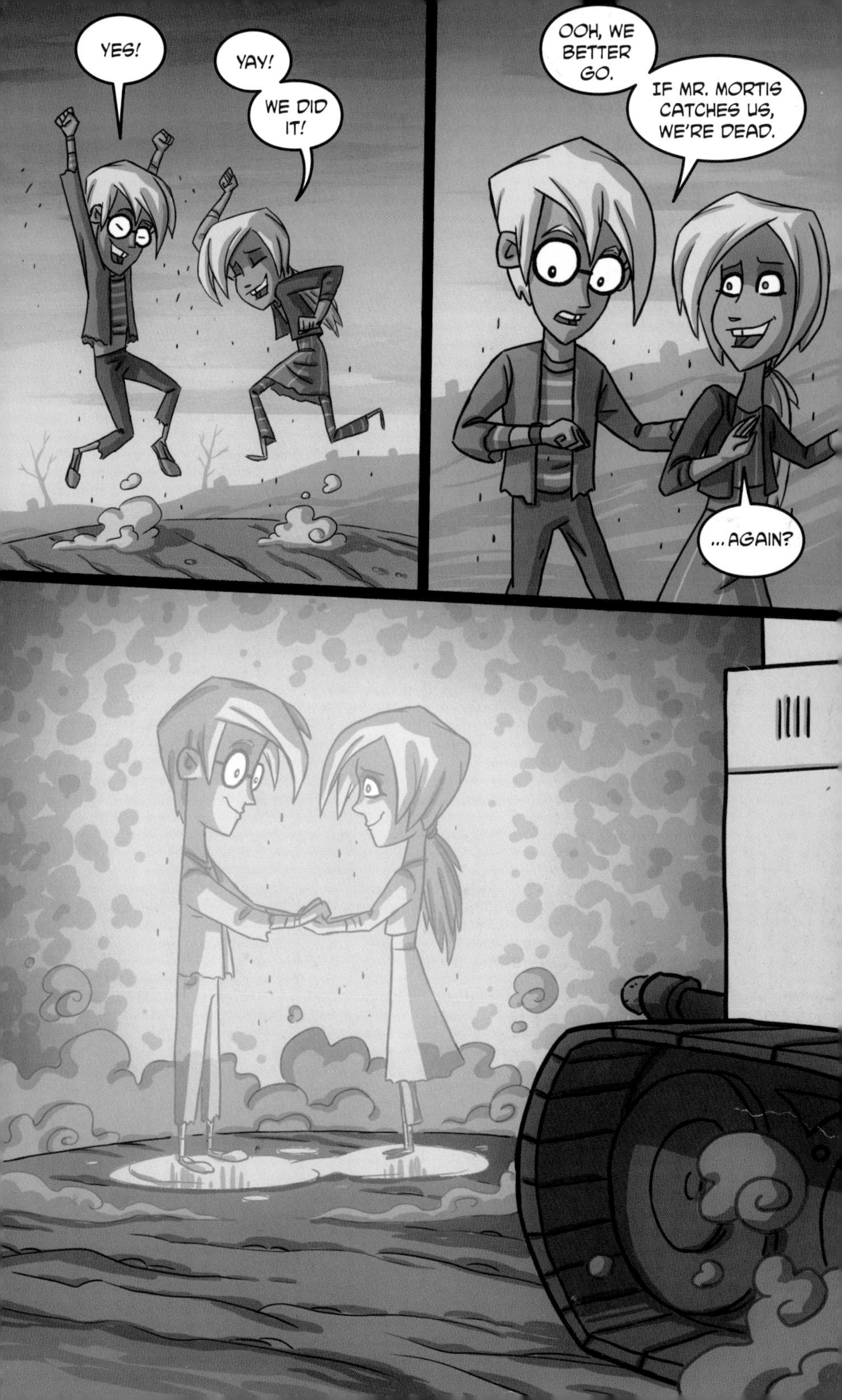
YES!
YAY!
WE DID IT!
OOH, WE BETTER GO.
IF MR. MORTIS CATCHES US, WE'RE DEAD.
...AGAIN?

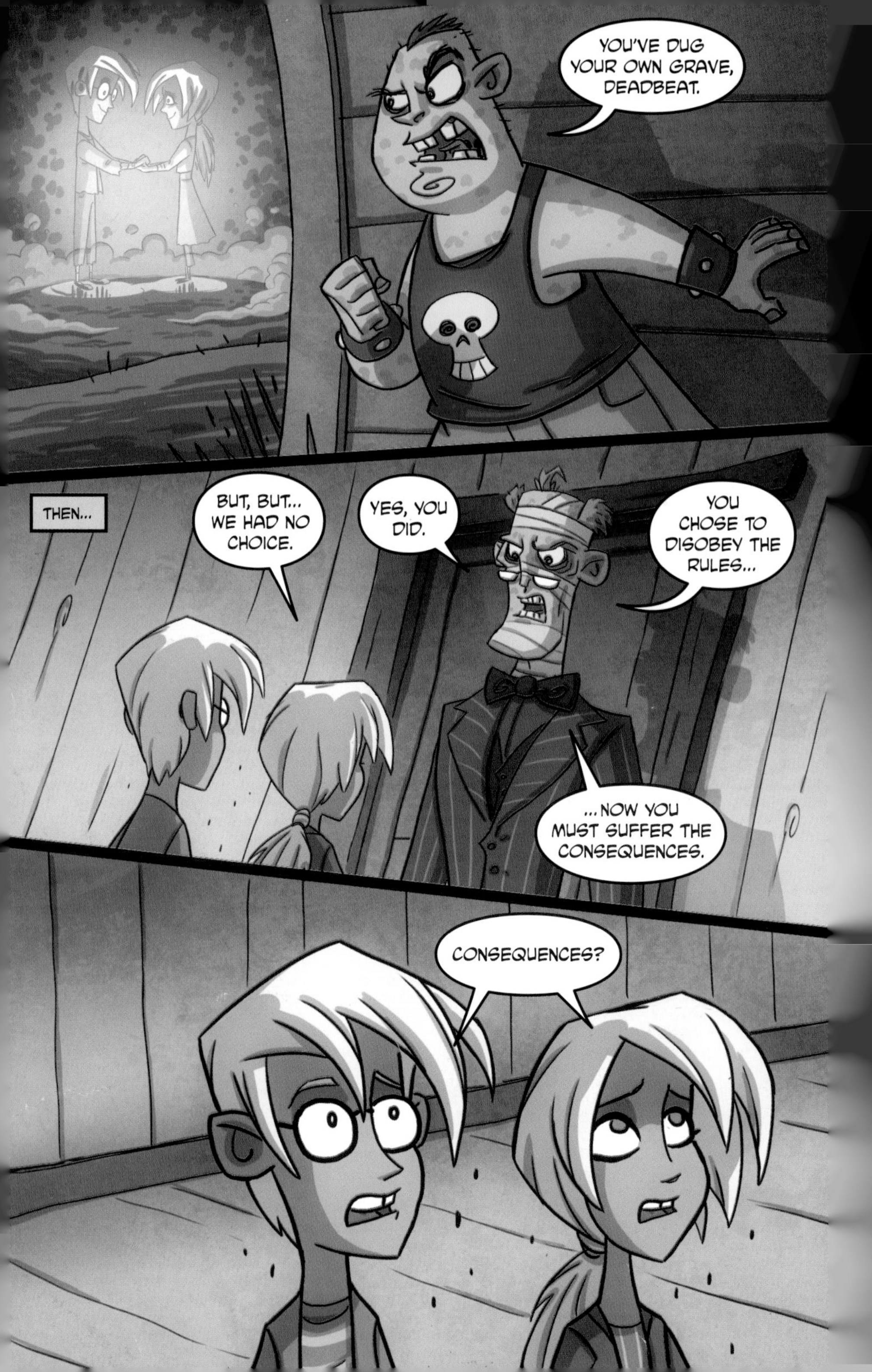
YOU'VE DUG YOUR OWN GRAVE, DEADBEAT.
THEN...
BUT, BUT... WE HAD NO CHOICE.
YES, YOU DID.
YOU CHOSE TO DISOBEY THE RULES...
...NOW YOU MUST SUFFER THE CONSEQUENCES.
CONSEQUENCES?

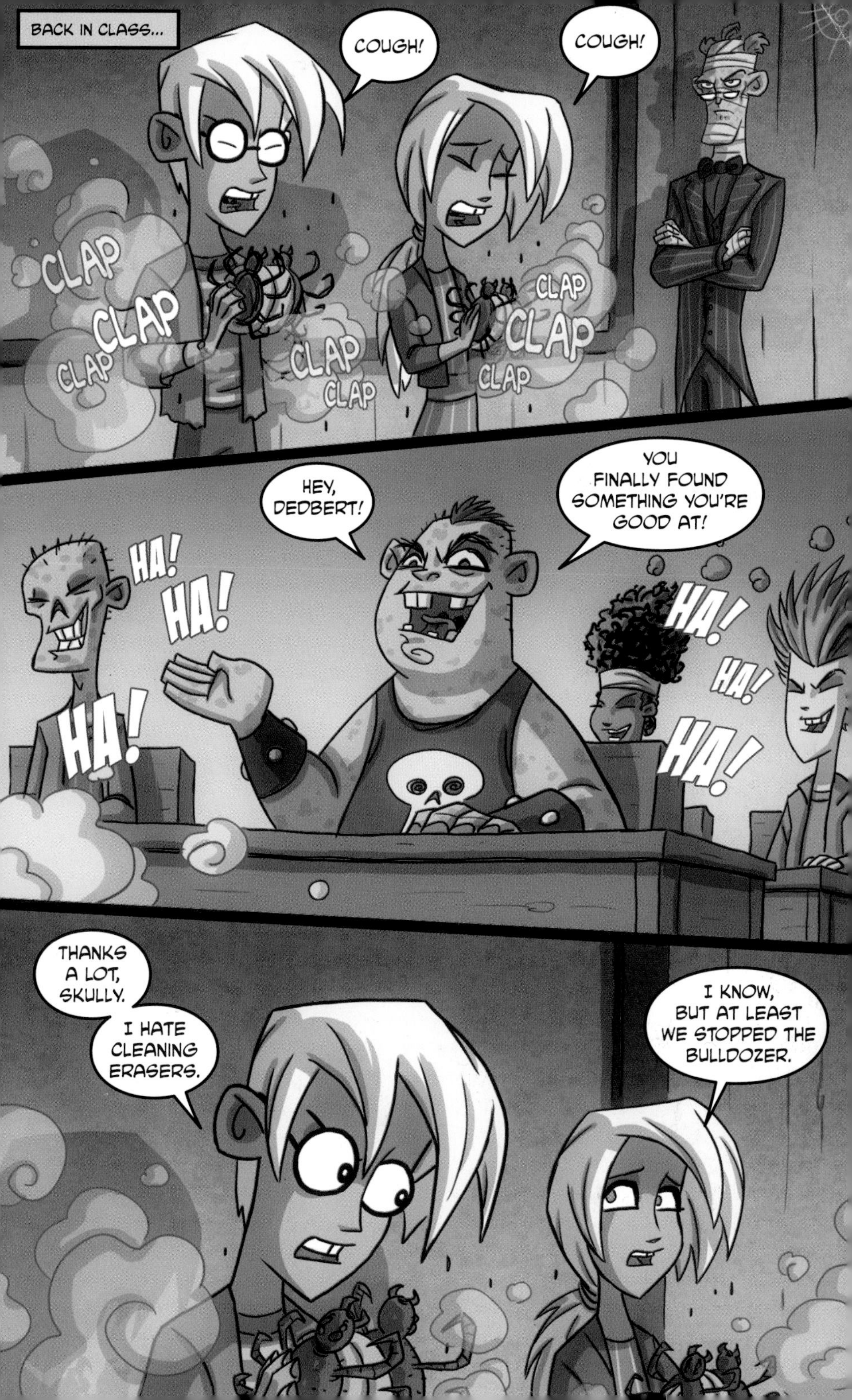
BACK IN CLASS...
COUGH!
COUGH!
CLAP CLAP CLAP CLAP CLAP
CLAP CLAP CLAP CLAP
HEY, DEDBERT!
YOU FINALLY FOUND SOMETHING YOU'RE GOOD AT!
HA! HA! HA!
HA! HA! HA!
THANKS A LOT, SKULLY.
I HATE CLEANING ERASERS.
I KNOW, BUT AT LEAST WE STOPPED THE BULLDOZER.

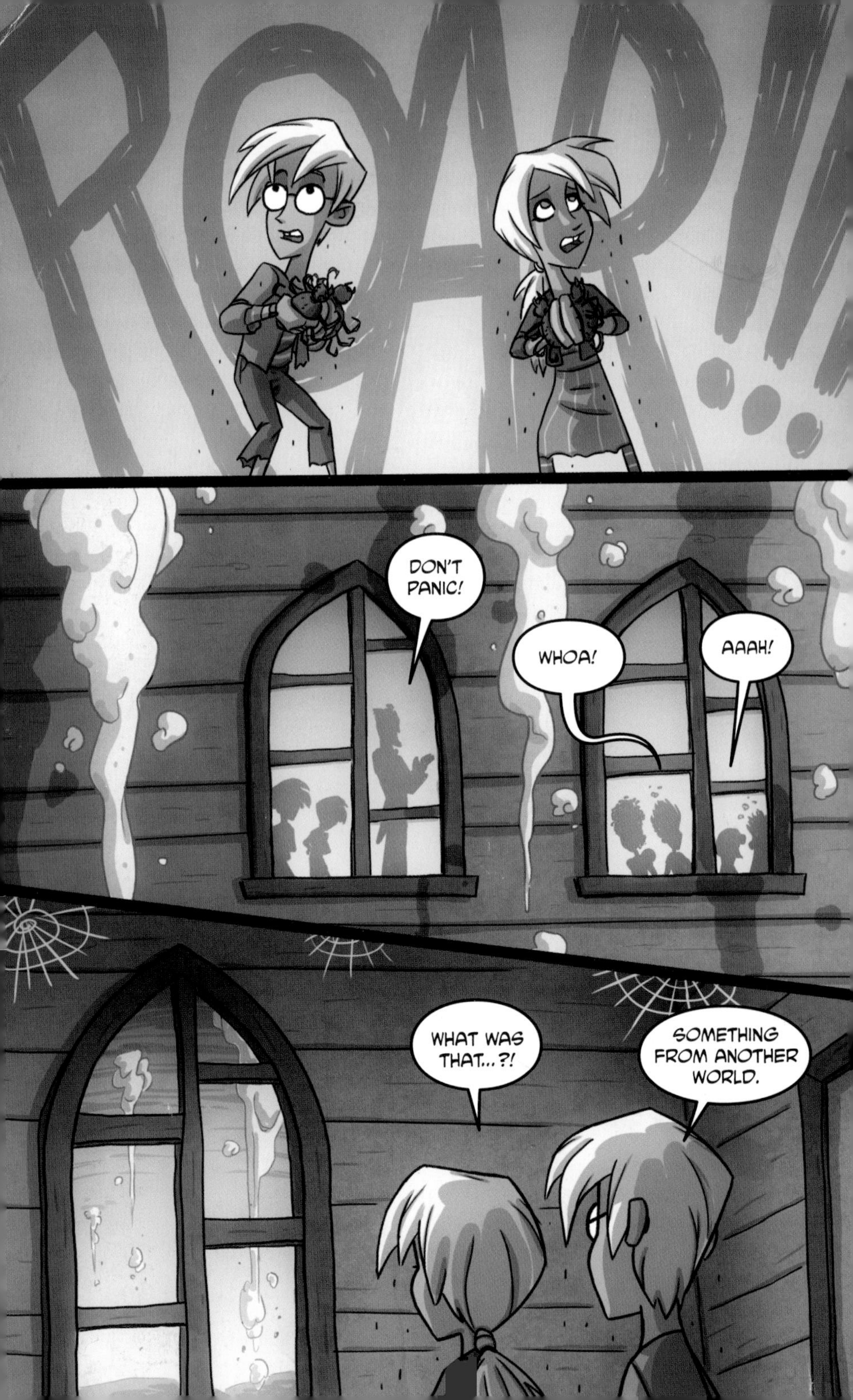
ROAR!...
DON'T PANIC!
WHOA!
AAAH!
WHAT WAS THAT...?!
SOMETHING FROM ANOTHER WORLD.

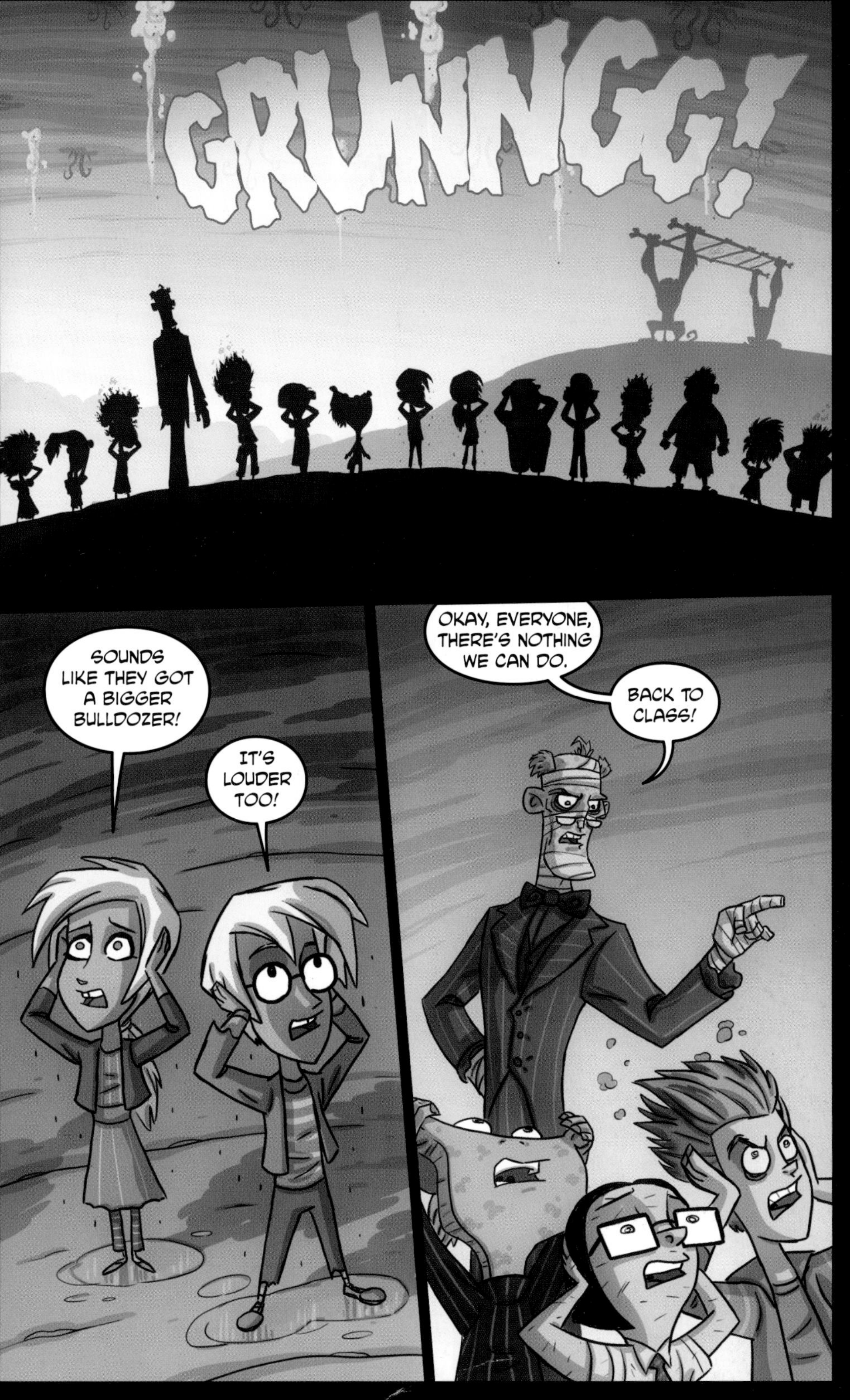
GRUNNGG!
SOUNDS LIKE THEY GOT A BIGGER BULLDOZER!
IT'S LOUDER TOO!
OKAY, EVERYONE, THERE'S NOTHING WE CAN DO.
BACK TO CLASS!

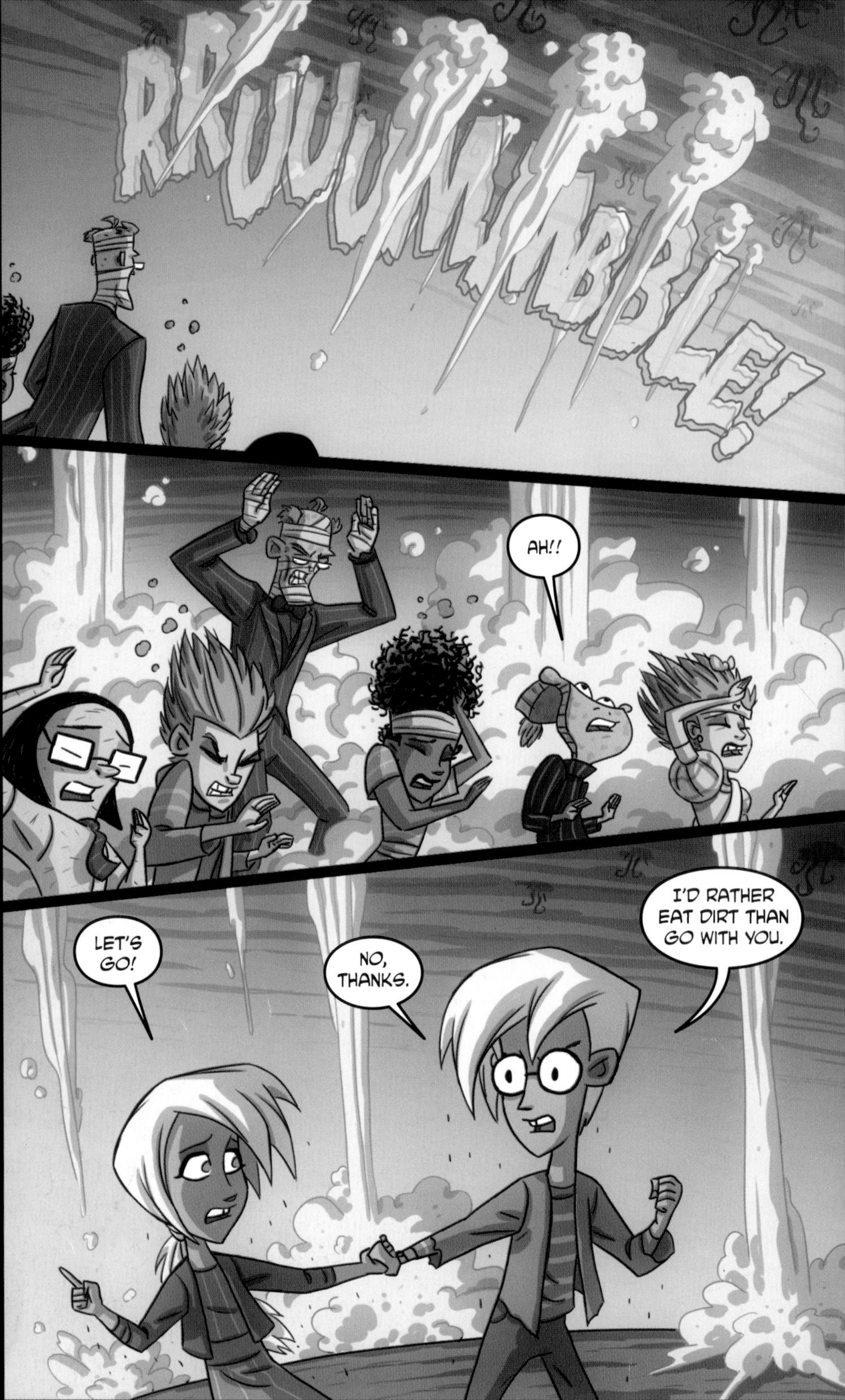
RRUUMMBBLE!
AH!!
LET'S GO!
NO, THANKS.
I'D RATHER EAT DIRT THAN GO WITH YOU.

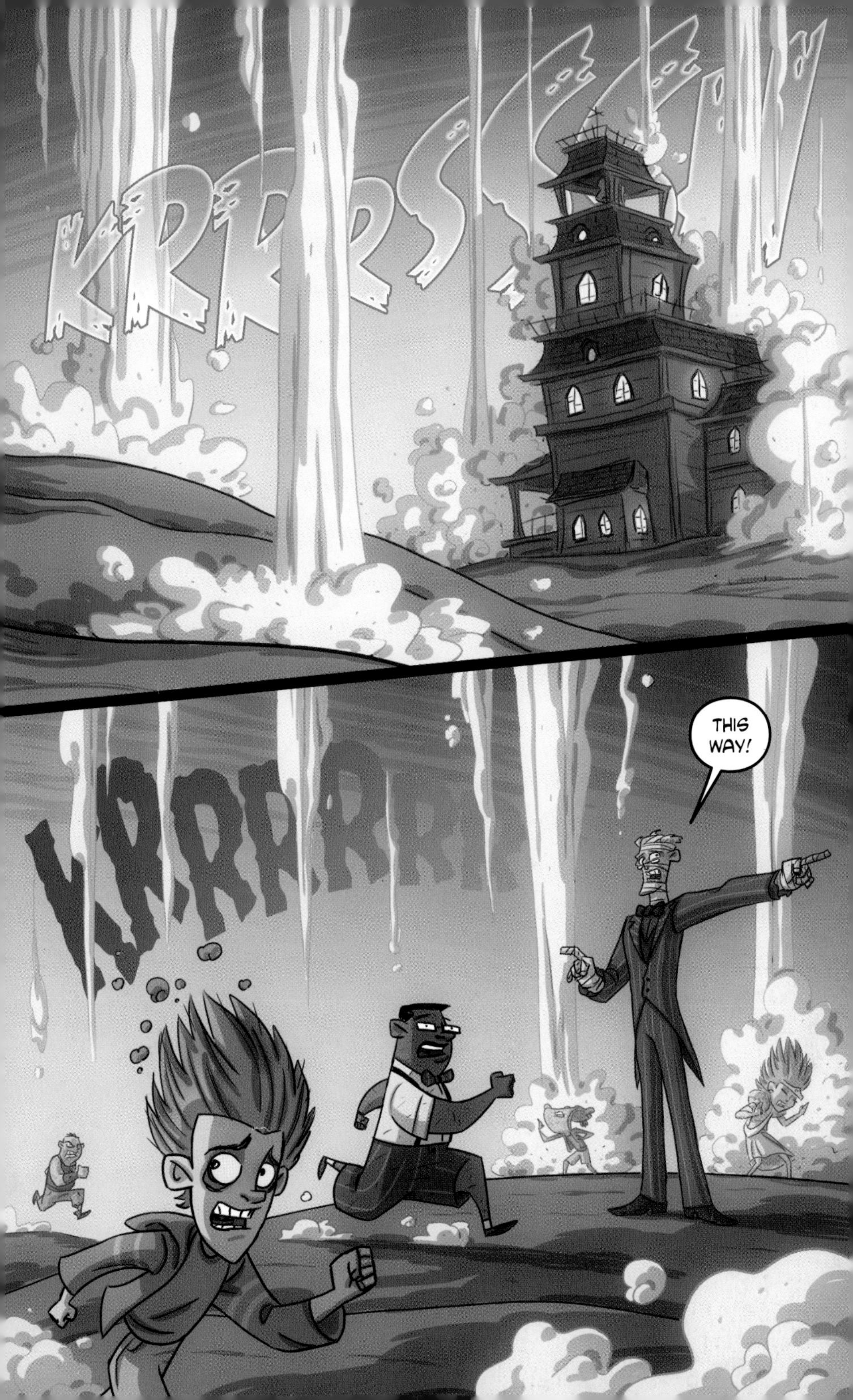
THIS WAY!

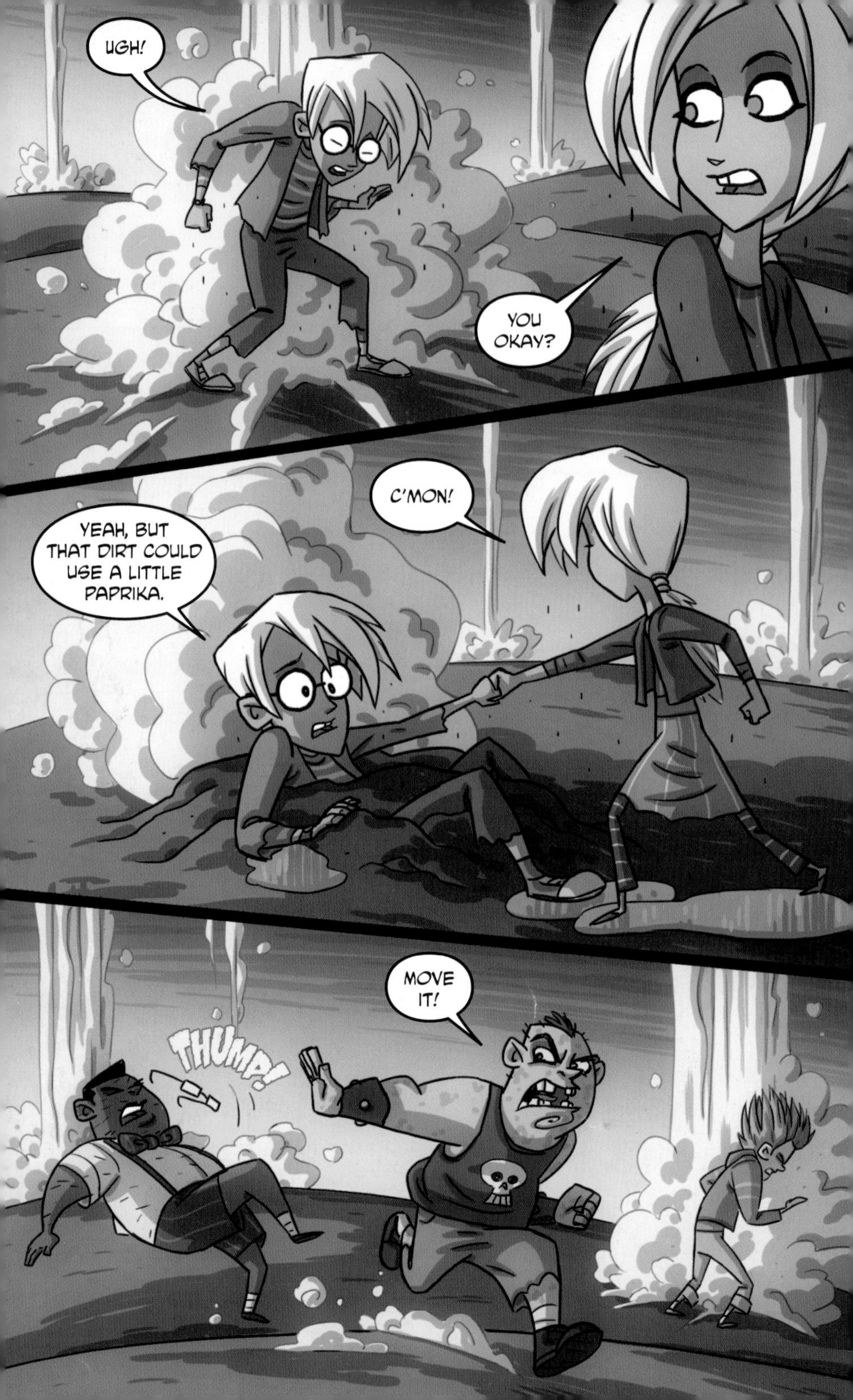
UGH!
YOU OKAY?
C'MON!
YEAH, BUT THAT DIRT COULD USE A LITTLE PAPRIKA.
MOVE IT!
THUMP!

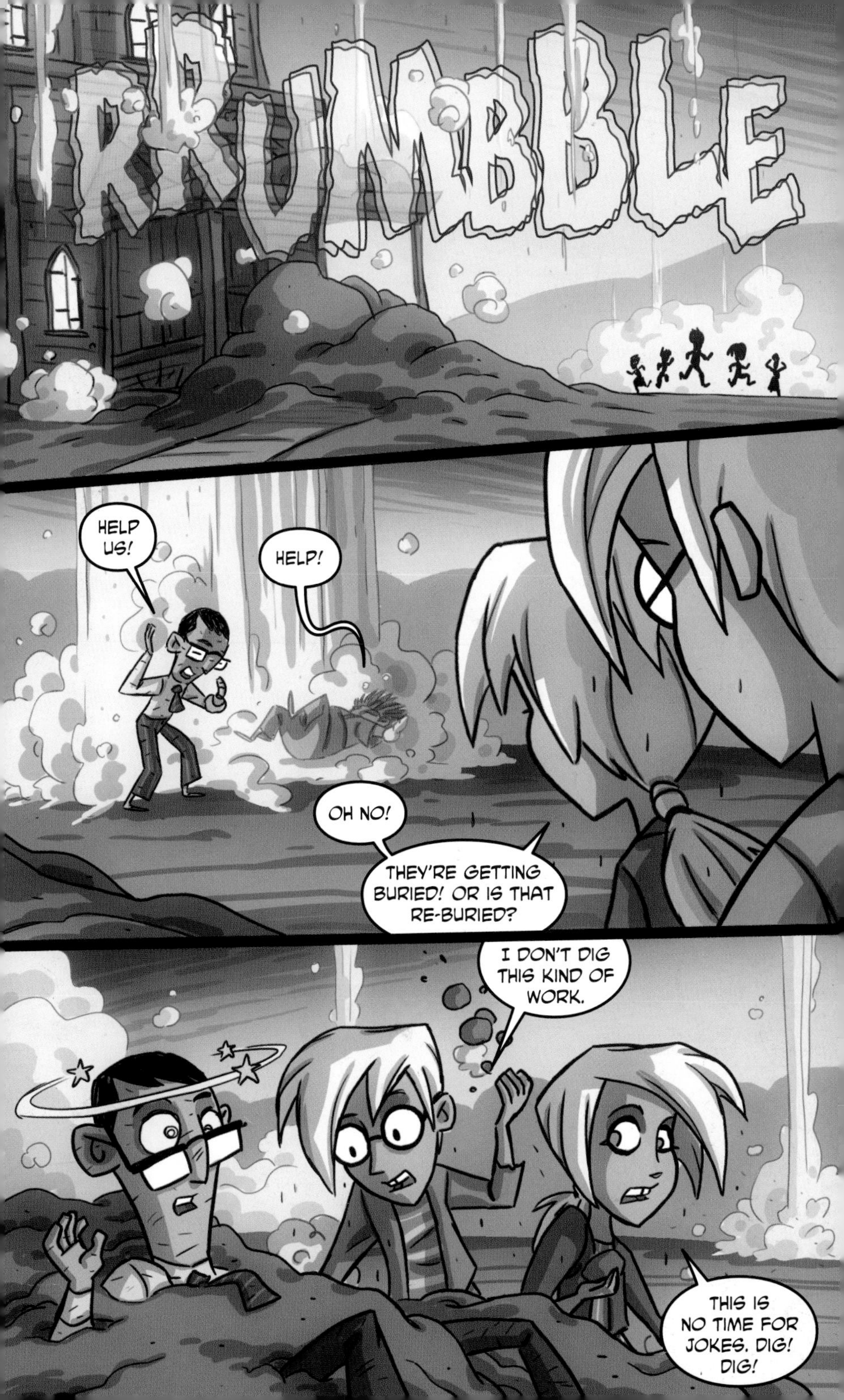
RUMBBLE
HELP US!
HELP!
OH NO!
THEY'RE GETTING BURIED! OR IS THAT RE-BURIED?
I DON'T DIG THIS KIND OF WORK.
THIS IS NO TIME FOR JOKES. DIG! DIG!

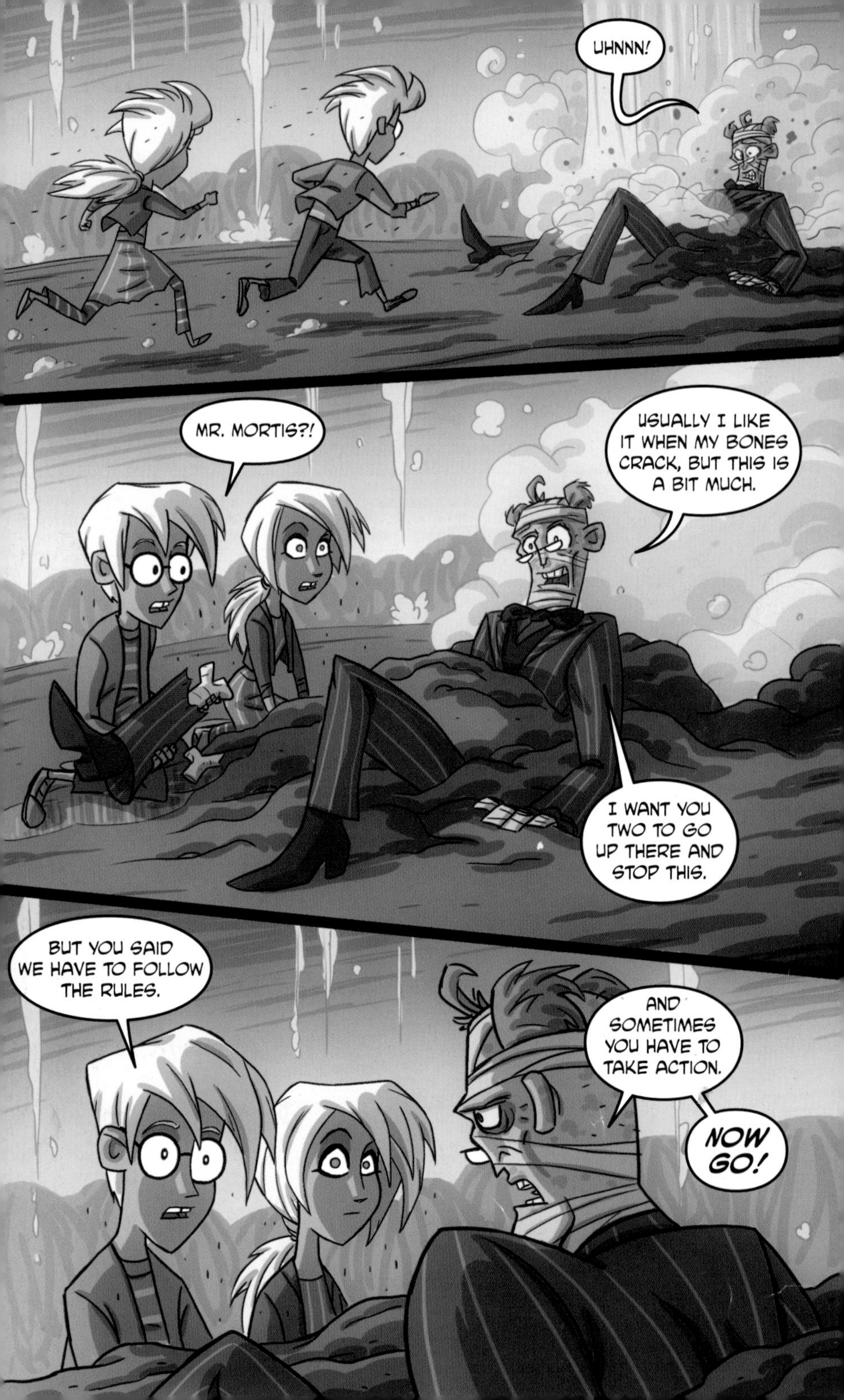
UHNNN!
MR. MORTIS?!
USUALLY I LIKE IT WHEN MY BONES CRACK, BUT THIS IS A BIT MUCH.
I WANT YOU TWO TO GO UP THERE AND STOP THIS.
BUT YOU SAID WE HAVE TO FOLLOW THE RULES.
AND SOMETIMES YOU HAVE TO TAKE ACTION.
NOW GO!

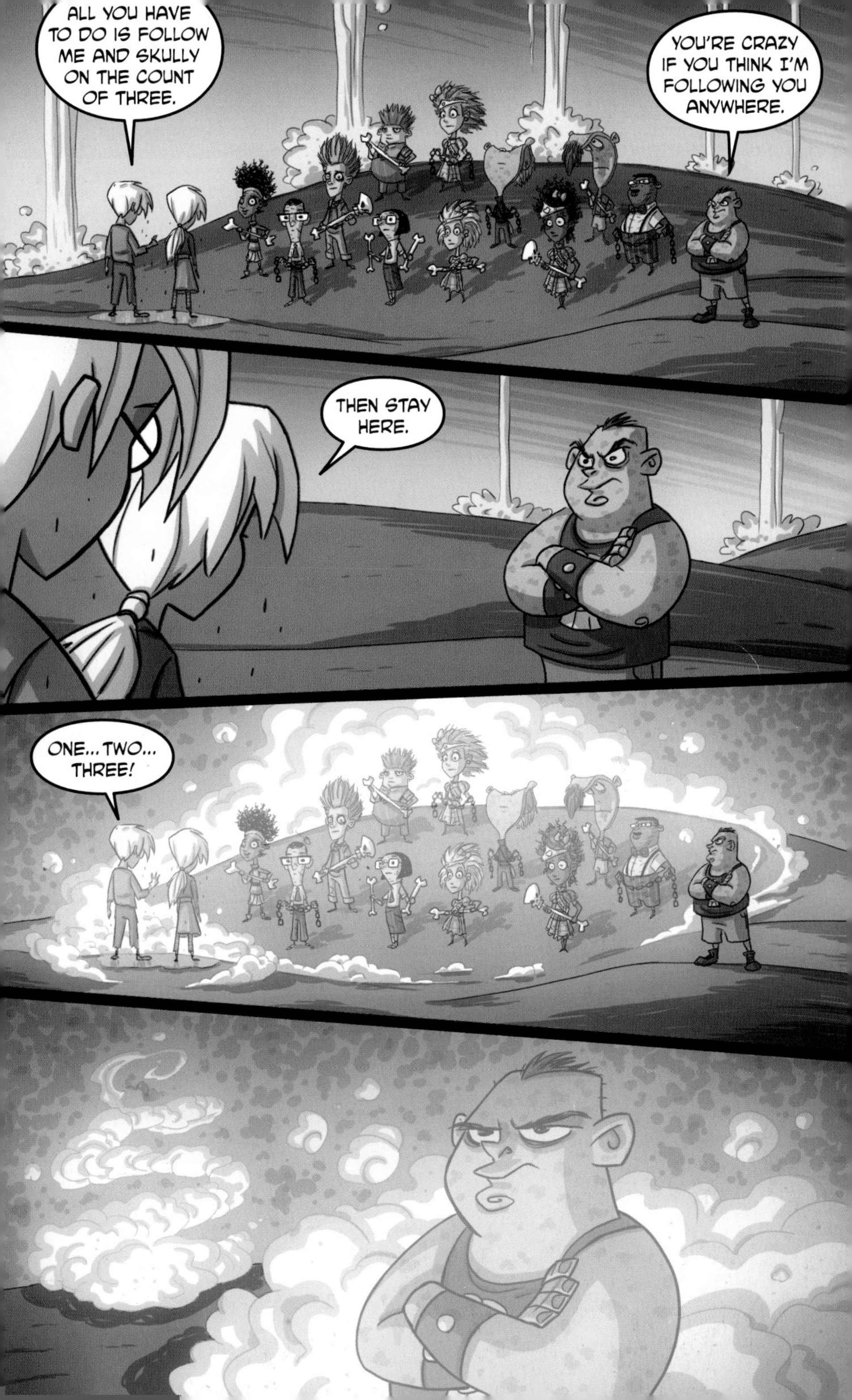

ALL YOU HAVE TO DO IS FOLLOW ME AND SKULLY ON THE COUNT OF THREE.
YOU'RE CRAZY IF YOU THINK I'M FOLLOWING YOU ANYWHERE.
THEN STAY HERE.
ONE... TWO... THREE!

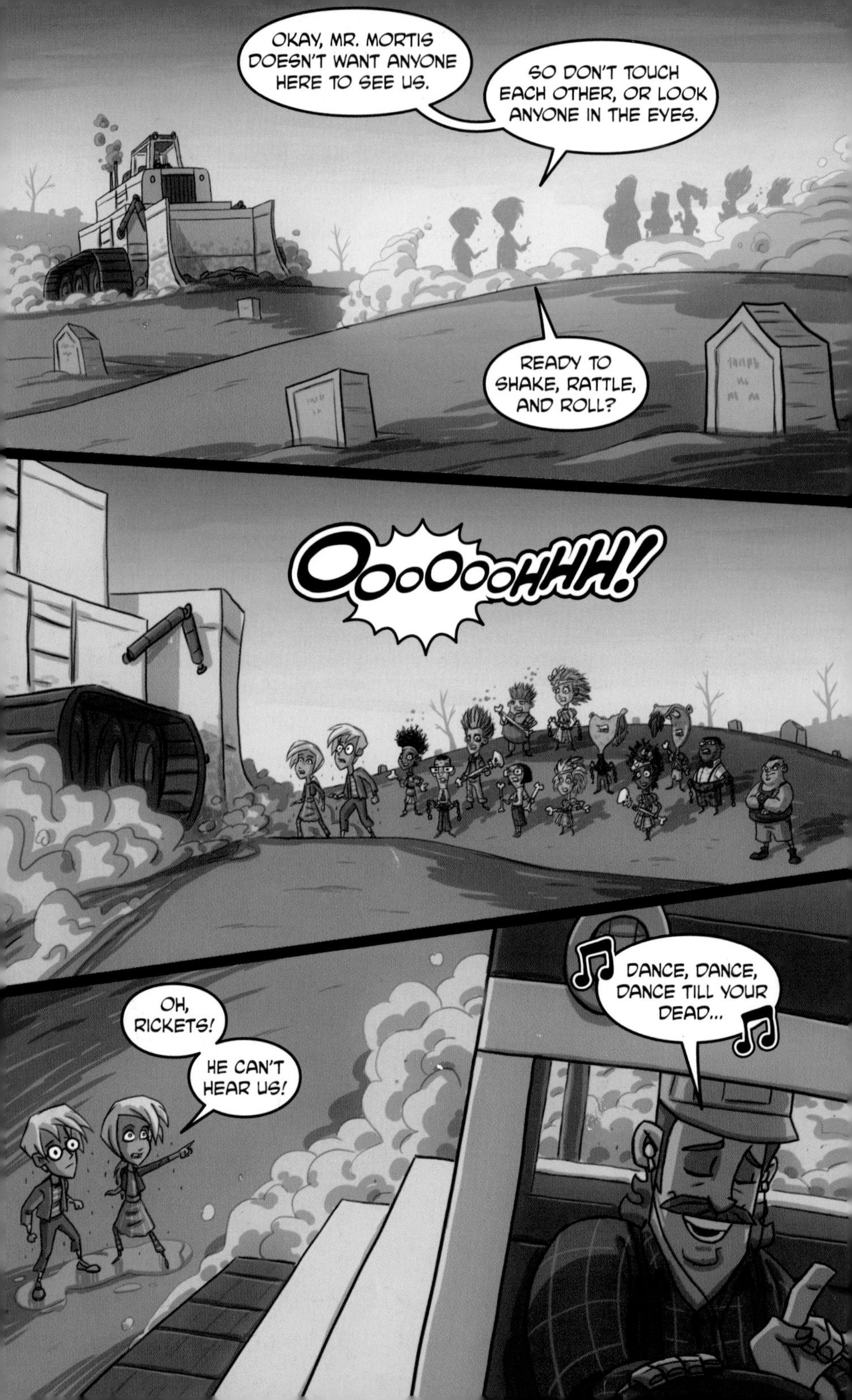
OKAY, MR. MORTIS DOESN'T WANT ANYONE HERE TO SEE US.
SO DON'T TOUCH EACH OTHER, OR LOOK ANYONE IN THE EYES.
READY TO SHAKE, RATTLE, AND ROLL?
OOOOOOOHHH!
OH, RICKETS!
HE CAN'T HEAR US!
DANCE, DANCE, DANCE TILL YOUR DEAD...

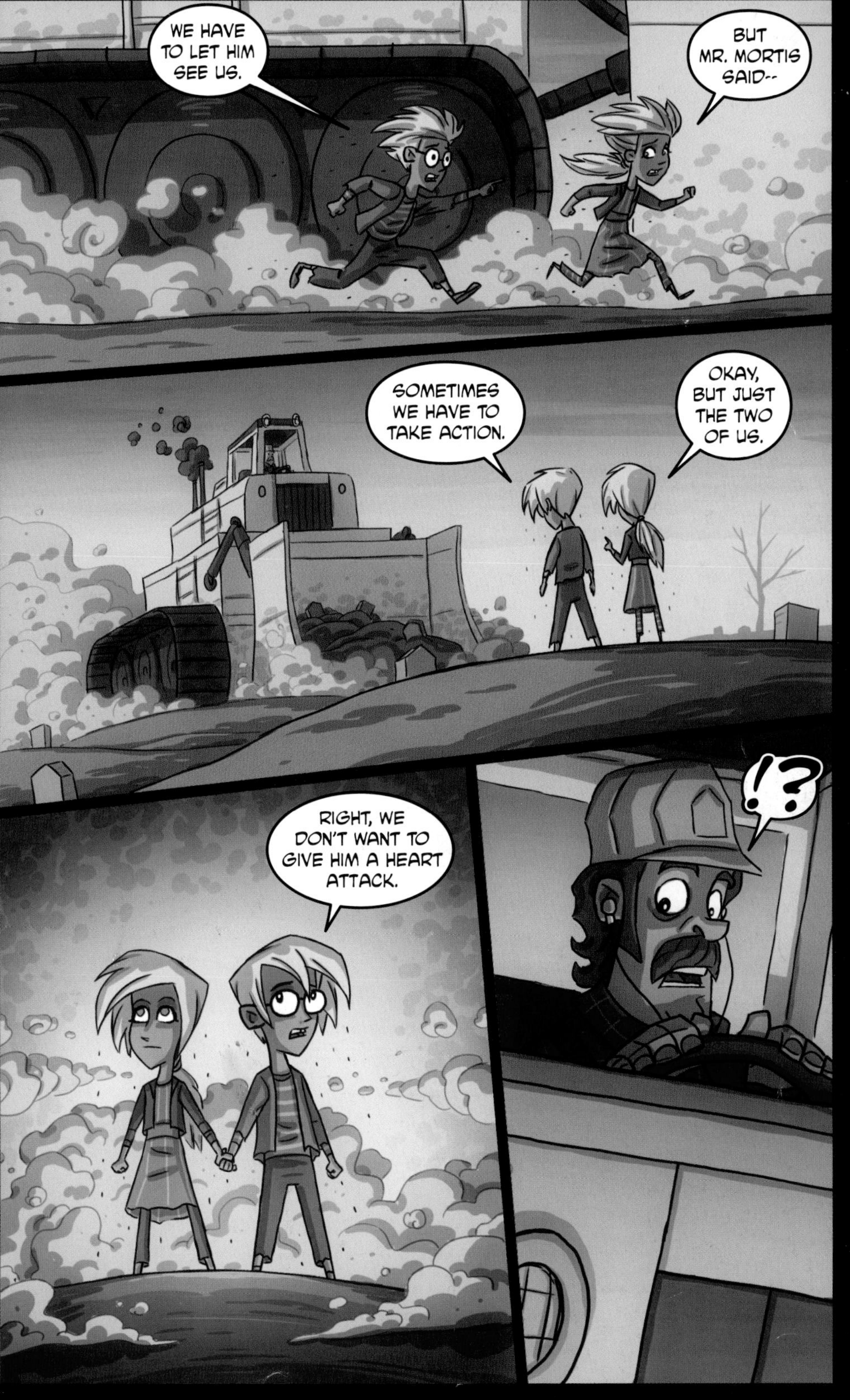
WE HAVE TO LET HIM SEE US.
BUT MR. MORTIS SAID--
SOMETIMES WE HAVE TO TAKE ACTION.
OKAY, BUT JUST THE TWO OF US.
RIGHT, WE DON'T WANT TO GIVE HIM A HEART ATTACK.
!?

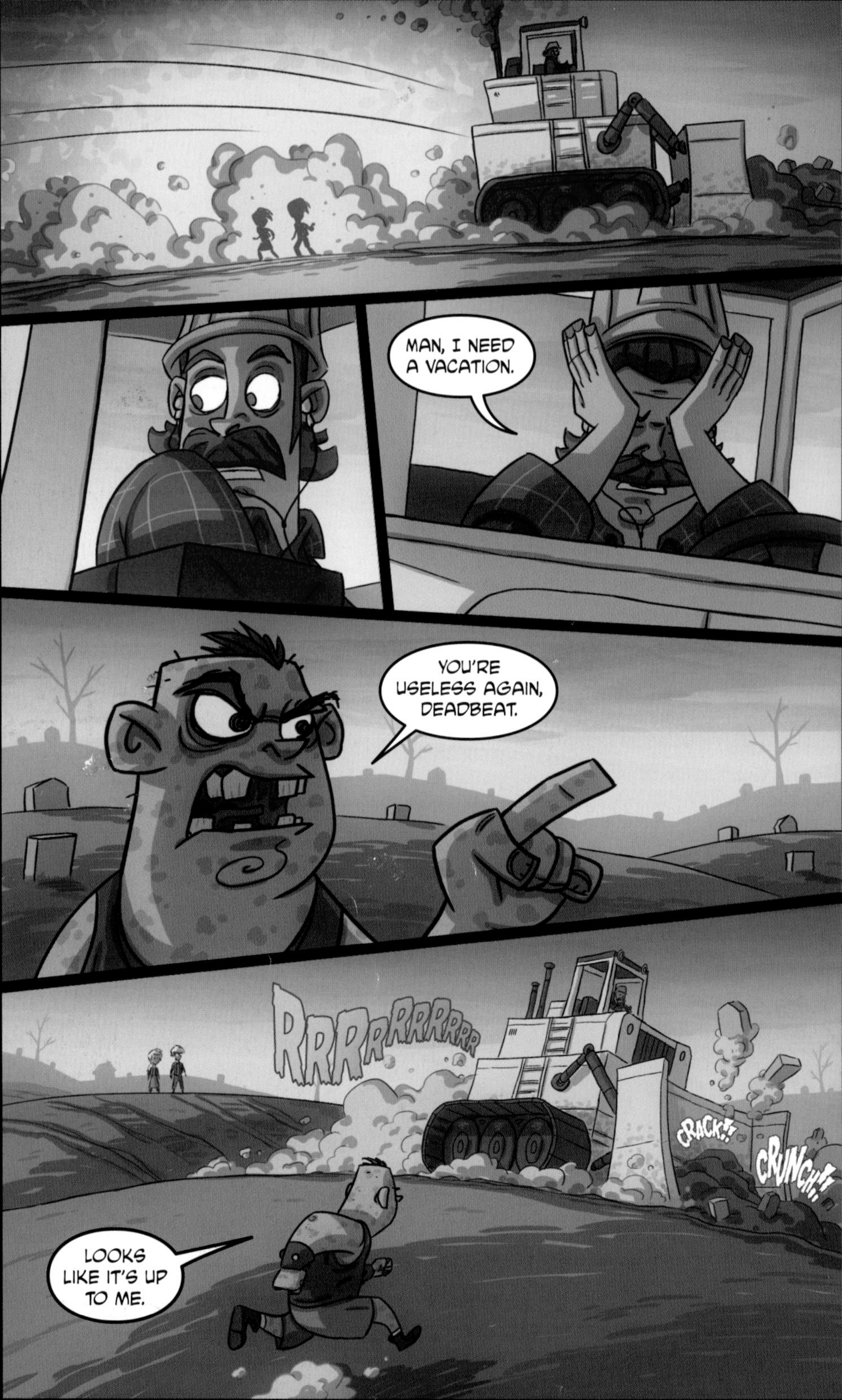
MAN, I NEED A VACATION.
YOU'RE USELESS AGAIN, DEADBEAT.
RRRRRRRRRRR
CRACK!!
CRUNCH!!
LOOKS LIKE IT'S UP TO ME.

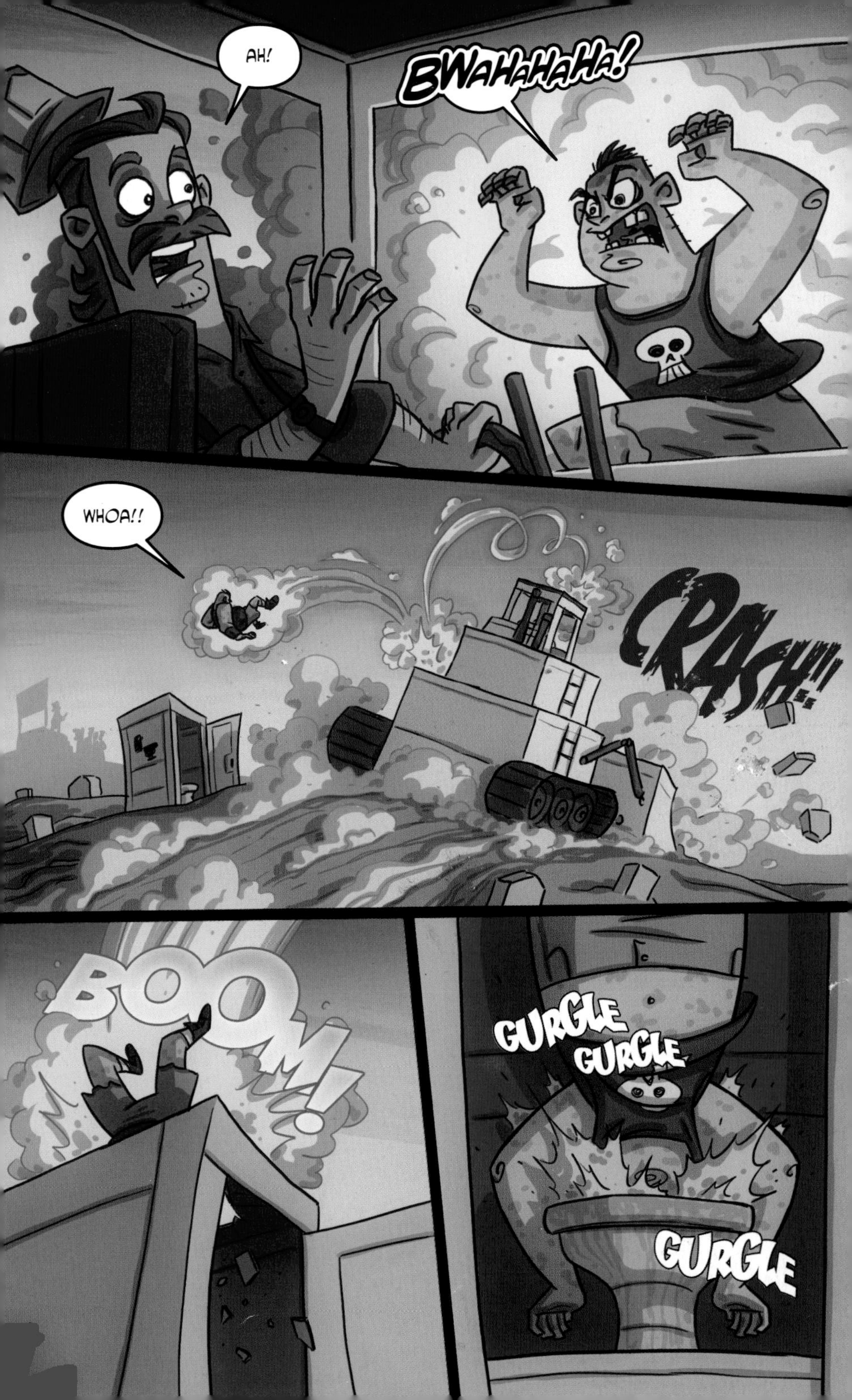
AH!
BWAHAHAHA!
WHOA!!
CRASH!!
BOOM!
GURGLE
GURGLE
GURGLE

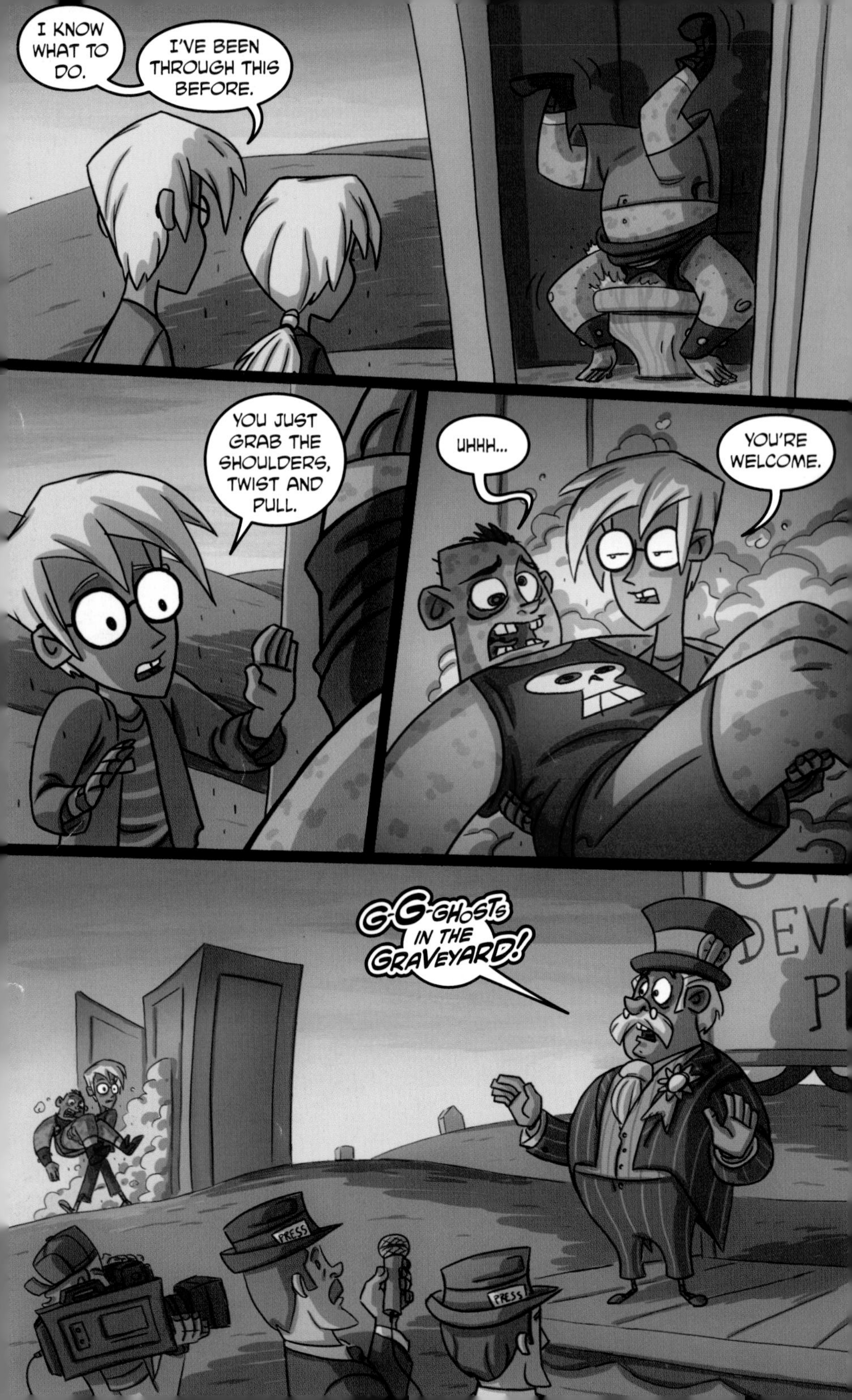
I KNOW WHAT TO DO.
I'VE BEEN THROUGH THIS BEFORE.
YOU JUST GRAB THE SHOULDERS, TWIST AND PULL.
UHHH...
YOU'RE WELCOME.
G-G-GHOSTS IN THE GRAVEYARD!
PRESS
PRESS

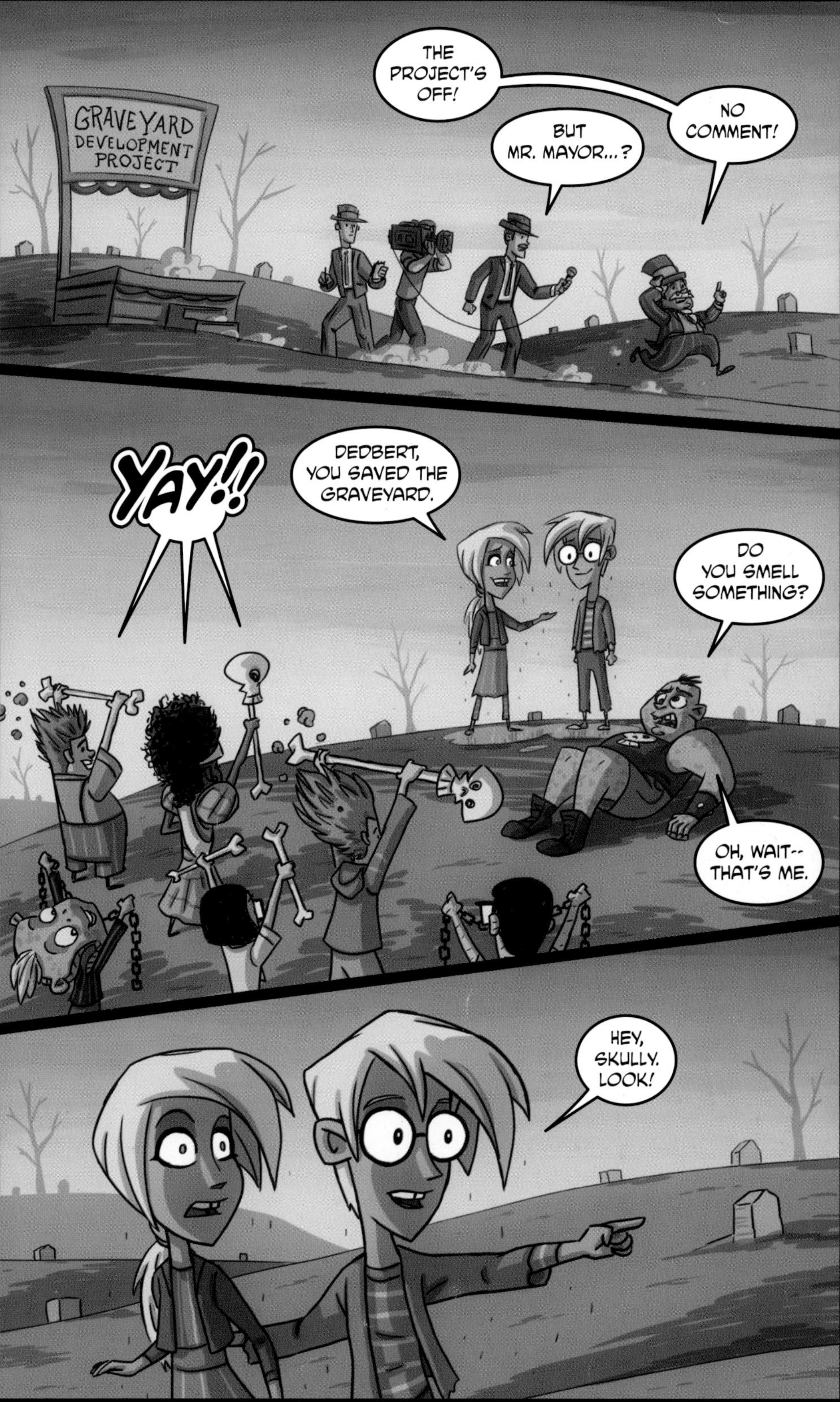
GRAVEYARD DEVELOPMENT PROJECT
THE PROJECT'S OFF!
BUT MR. MAYOR...?
NO COMMENT!
YAY!!
DEDBERT, YOU SAVED THE GRAVEYARD.
DO YOU SMELL SOMETHING?
OH, WAIT-- THAT'S ME.
HEY, SKULLY. LOOK!

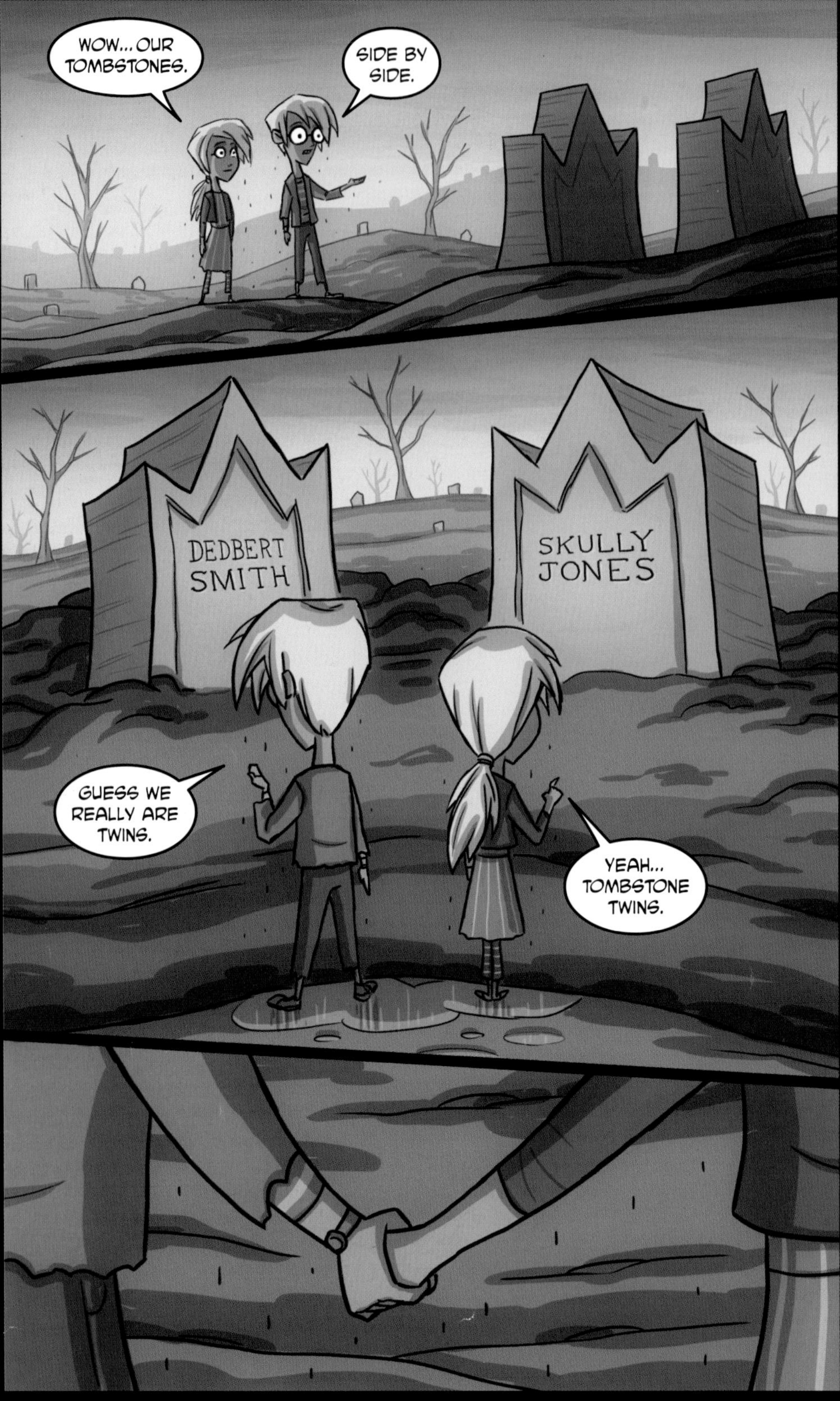
WOW... OUR TOMBSTONES.
SIDE BY SIDE.
DEDBERT SMITH
SKULLY JONES
GUESS WE REALLY ARE TWINS.
YEAH... TOMBSTONE TWINS.

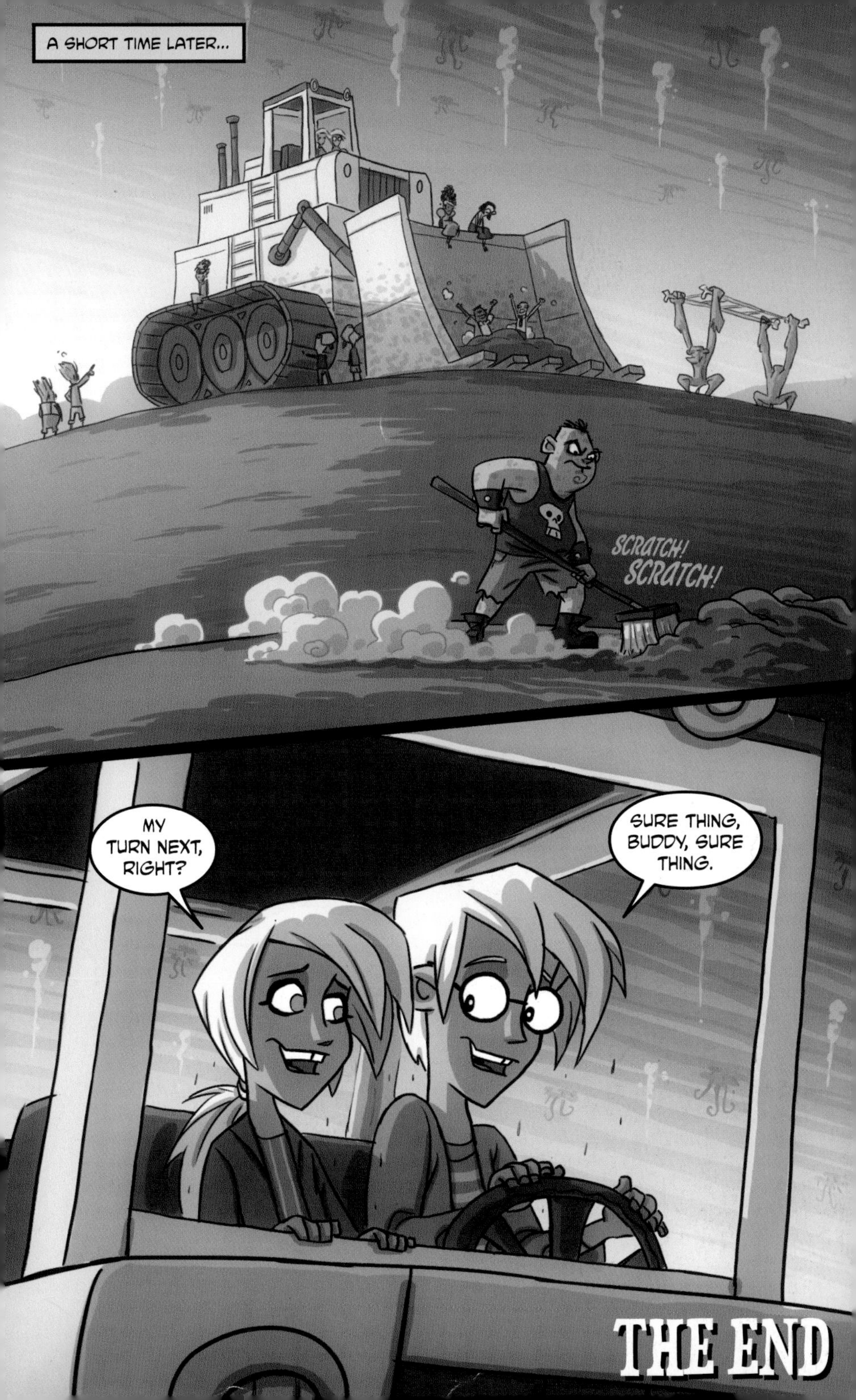
A SHORT TIME LATER...
SCRATCH! SCRATCH!
MY TURN NEXT, RIGHT?
SURE THING, BUDDY, SURE THING.
THE END

CREATORS

DENISE DOWNER

Denise Downer is a children's animation and graphic novel writer from Los Angeles, California. She has written shows on today's top networks, including Fox, Nickelodeon, and Cartoon Network. Her credits include The Bernie Mac Show, All Grown Up, Pink Panther and Pals, Aaahh!!! Real Monsters, and other popular television series.

OTIS FRAMPTON

Writer, artist, and creator Otis Frampton was hatched in 1972 in Memphis, Tennessee (he quickly flew that particular coop and became a Minnesota Yankee). His interest in illustration began at a very early age, and his first medium was "butter-on-carpet". Unfortunately, that masterpiece is no longer available for public viewing, as his mother was his first critic, and quickly eliminated all evidence of his early genius. Years later, his passion for creating fantastic imagery remains as strong as ever (as does his love of butter). He is the creator of the Oddly Normal graphic novel series, and has illustrated many of today's top properties, including Star Wars, The Avengers, Lord of the Rings, and more.

GLOSSARY

asphalt (ASS-fawlt)—a black, tarlike substance that is mixed with sand and gravel and then rolled flat to make roads

board (BORD)—a group of people who control a company or committee

concentrate (KON-suhn-trate)—to focus your thoughts and attention on something

consequence (KON-suh-kwenss)—the result of an action

disobey (diss-oh-BAY)—to go against the rules

grave (GRAYV)—a very serious situation; also, a place where a dead person is buried.

jock (JOK)—a slang term for an athlete

paprika (pa-PREEK-uh)—a reddish orange spice made from powdered sweet red peppers

pedestal (PED-i-stuhl)—a base for a statue; if you put someone on a pedestal, you admire and respect the person excessively.

socked (SOKD)—hit someone very hard

suffer (SUHF-ur)—to experience or undergo something unpleasant

VISUAL QUESTIONS

1. The Tombstone Twins worked together to save the day. Do you think either of them could've solved the Underworld's problem alone? Why or why not?

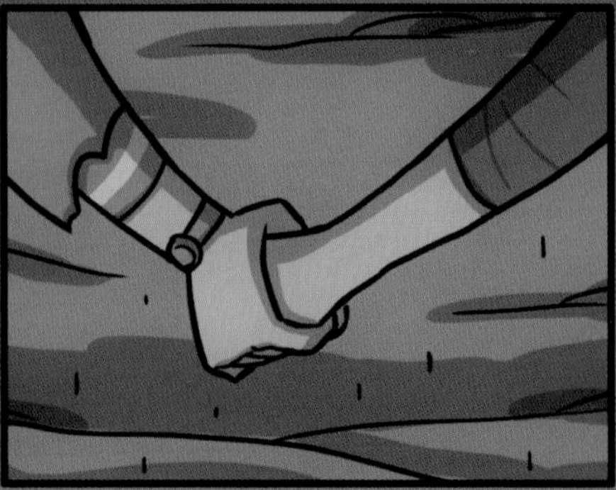

2. The way a character's eyes and mouth look, also known as their facial expression, can tell a lot about the emotions he or she is feeling. In the image below, how do you think Dedbert is feeling?

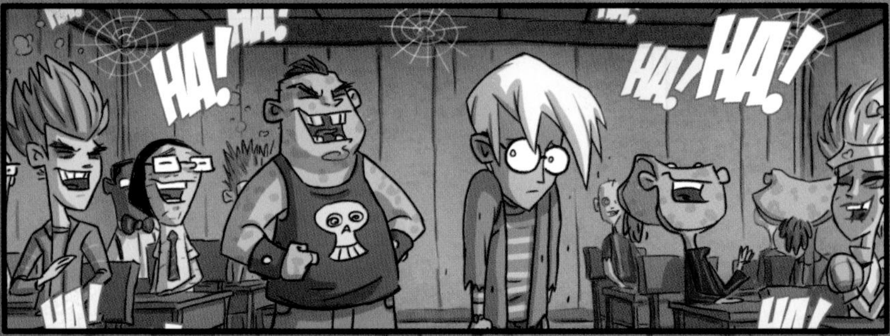
HA!
HA!
HA!
HA!

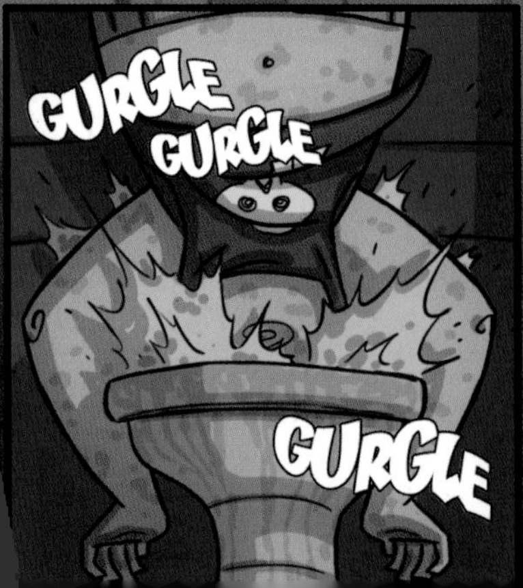
GURGLE
GURGLE
GURGLE

3. In comic books, sound effects (also known as SFX) are used to show sounds. Make a list of all the sound effects in this book, and then write a definition for each term. Soon, you'll have your own SFX dictionary!

4. A pun is a joke based on one word that has two meanings, such as Mr. Mortis' use of the word "grave" on page 16. Find other puns in this book, and then try making up a few of your own.

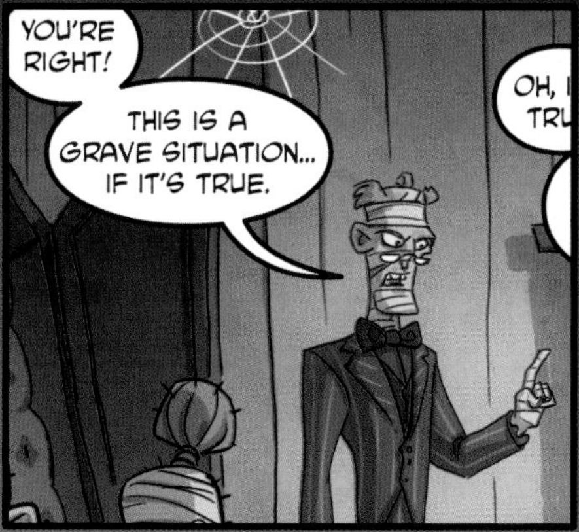
YOU'RE RIGHT!
THIS IS A GRAVE SITUATION... IF IT'S TRUE.

5. Create your own character to star in the next Tombstone Twins book. What is their name? What do they look like? Write a few paragraphs about your character, then draw a picture of him or her.

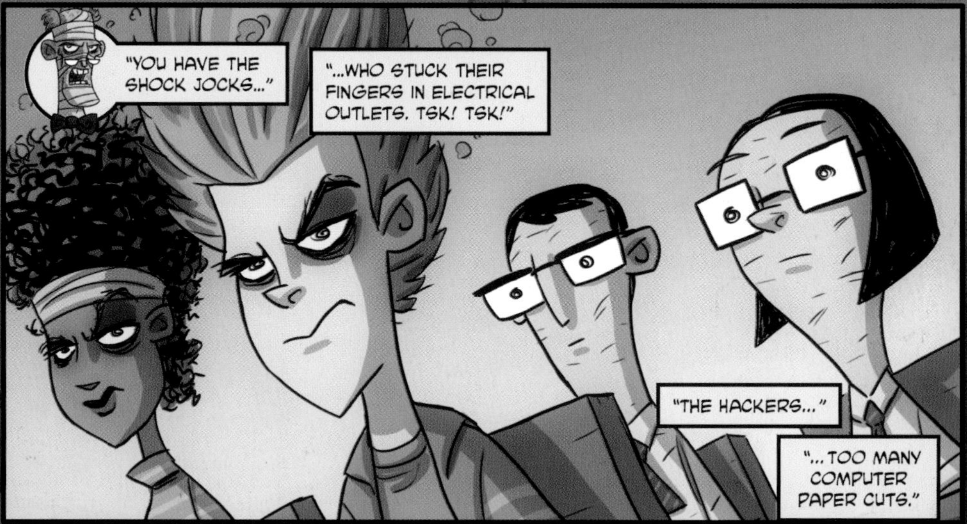
"YOU HAVE THE SHOCK JOCKS..."
"...WHO STUCK THEIR FINGERS IN ELECTRICAL OUTLETS. TSK! TSK!"
"THE HACKERS..."
"...TOO MANY COMPUTER PAPER CUTS."

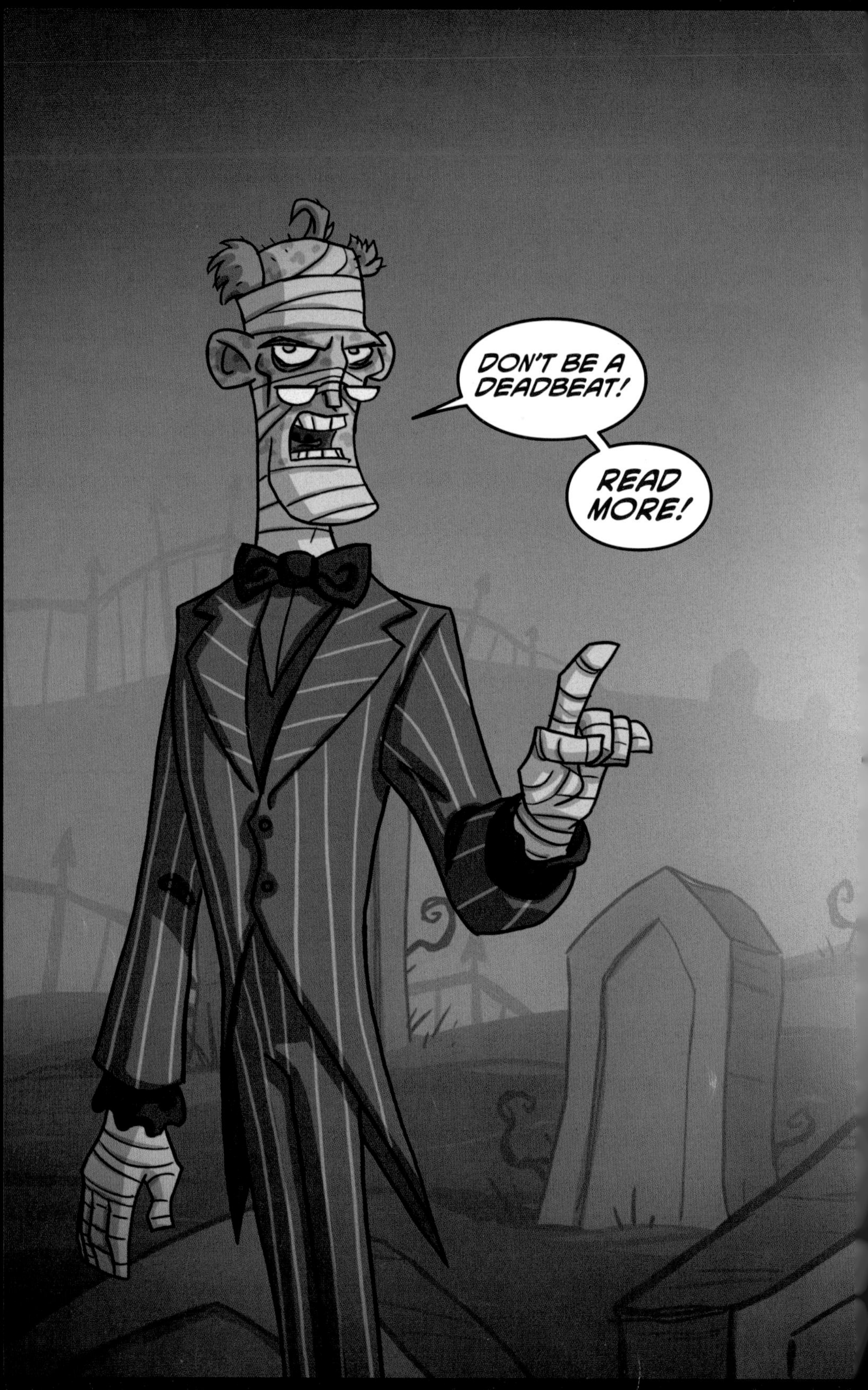
DON'T BE A DEADBEAT!
READ MORE!

LOOK FOR OTHER GREAT STORIES!

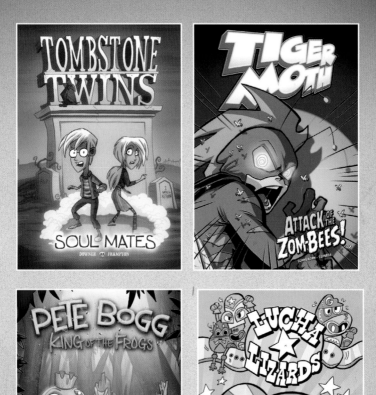

THE FUN DOESN'T STOP HERE!

DISCOVER MORE AT...

WWW.CAPSTONEKIDS.COM

FIND COOL WEBSITES AND MORE BOOKS LIKE THIS ONE AT WWW.FACTHOUND.COM.

JUST TYPE IN THE BOOK ID: 9781434222480 AND YOU'RE READY TO GO!

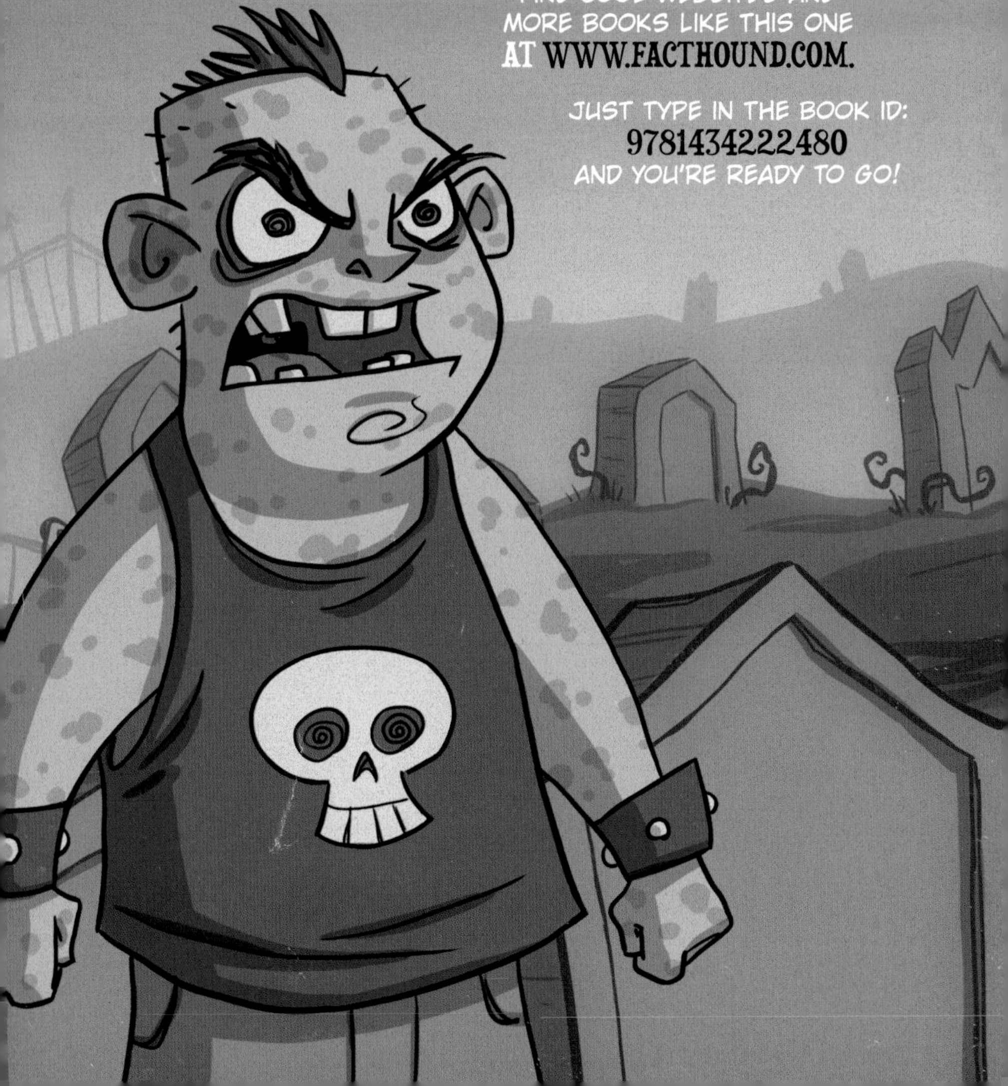